GIDEON'S
HOUSE

Also by Jean Brody

THE TWENTY YEAR PHENOMENON
(with Gail Boswick Osborne)

GIDEON'S HOUSE

JEAN BRODY

G. P. Putnam's Sons
New York

I owe a debt of gratitude to the many journalists—in particular, John McCormally—through whose eyes I have witnessed tornados.

Designed by Richard Oriolo

Library of Congress Cataloging in Publication Data

Brody, Jean.
Gideon's house.

I. Title.
PS3552.R625G5   1984   813'.54   83-17839
ISBN 0-399-12937-5

Printed in the United States of America
Second Impression

*For my father
and the memory of my mother*

Seldom, very seldom does complete truth belong to any human disclosure; seldom can it happen that something is not a little disguised or a little mistaken.

—JANE AUSTEN

GIDEON'S
HOUSE

ONE

PAGE GARRITY found his grandmother in the attic, slumped and skewed like an oversize rag doll, in an old rattan rocker; yellowed, scalloped-edge photographs scattered at her feet, spilling from her lap, clutched in her hands.

Wagging his head in disgust, he made his way down the stairs to the study, where he pushed open the door with his foot and stood, thumbs hooked through the loops of his Levi's, in the doorway. He waited, relishing his news, turning over in his mind how he would tell it, debating as to which sort of telling would most annoy his mother. He settled on rudeness. She could not abide rudeness.

"Guess what?" A good opening, he thought, a slightly breathy rendering, tinged with the promise of a minor disaster.

"What is it?" she murmured absently, not looking up from the stack of test papers in front of her.

He would wait a little longer; a few more empty seconds to get her going.

"I'm busy, Page. What is it?"

He drew in a deep breath and announced cheerfully, "She's juiced again!"

Kate dropped the red pen which had just drawn an X over the word "mitosis" and printed neatly in the margin, "See diagram on pg. 144." She sighed. "How bad?"

"Out of it—swacked, bombed, totaled—"

"All right, that's enough," she interrupted sharply. She raised her hand to her forehead and ran her fingers over the ridges of a deep frown. She sighed again, then rose and moved decisively around the desk. "Go get your dad," she told him. He leaned against the doorjamb, making no move to follow her instructions, no effort to disguise his pleasure in the situation. "And be quick about it," she added.

He straightened tall out of his slouch, which, along with the heels on his cowboy boots, caused her to have to look up at him. "How come you let her stay here, anyway?"

She stared at him with hard, flat eyes, a stare he met and held as she walked past him, then she whirled suddenly and grasped his arm with one hand, the fingers digging in. "*Now*, Page," she commanded, and without looking back she climbed the stairs to the attic.

The door was open, and even before she moved across the room and knelt by the rocker Kate knew that this time was different. This was not the floating island, the rosy patch of nothingness, to which her mother so often fled. This was different.

"Momma?" Kate whispered. "Momma?"

Her eyes were closed, her chin rested on her shoulder, and a heavy sweep of autumn-brown hair fell across her face: thick but silken hair, rich with golden glints and the sudden fire of sun and shadow; the only remaining testimony to earlier beauty.

"Momma, it's all right. It'll be all right." She patted the thin, clenched hand, carefully removed a crumpled photograph and glanced at it in surprise, all the while crooning a litany, "It's all right . . . it's all right. . ."

At thirteen, Page's acts of disobedience had finite limits in time wherein he knew, almost to the second, how long his sullenness would be tolerated before privileges were revoked, how much longer before penance was imposed, and finally that exact moment when real punishment was in order. On this day, bright, crisp, and poised on the brink of a long weekend, he decided to take no more chances. As soon as the sound of his mother's footsteps had faded, he hurried to the stables, where he found his father and told him—quickly, respectfully, and with profound concern—of what had happened.

Moments later, Jason Garrity carried his mother-in-law to the room that had been hers again this past year, and laid her gently on the carved mahogany bed where she had conceived and borne her daughters more than three decades before. Long-dead geese had furnished the down for the mattress that received her. Gran Warwick's fine hand had set the pieces in the quilt with which he covered her. Three generations of Warwick women were there—the living, the dead and the dying—sewn in with tight, hidden stitches. Gran's canning apron with its orchard of stains. And here, a pinafore Kate had worn as a child. There, Susannah's fairy costume from a Christmas play. And scattered throughout, the silks and satins their mother was forever discarding and leaving behind in the ragbag on her brief and infrequent visits to the farm. All there: the soft worn cotton of Gran, the crisp gingham of Kate, the dotted swiss of Susannah, and the desperate shining fabric of Elizabeth. Commemorative diamonds.

As Kate watched Billy Harris move a stethoscope over her mother's chest, she reached for Jason's hand but, when he gave it, suddenly and in flushed confusion withdrew her own.

"It's a stroke," Billy said, "no question of that. A bad one." He licked his lips and lowered his voice to a sickroom whisper. "I doubt if she'll regain consciousness, but in any case in my opinion we shouldn't move her."

"But she's much too young to have a stroke," protested Kate, in whose mind strokes fell on musty widows, moldering with age and lack of use, not on the likes of her mother who came and went with the wind like a migratory bird blown off course.

Billy shook his head and touched her shoulder. "Your momma has lived her life with her foot flat out on the floorboards, you know that. A body has got just so much mileage in it." He shook his head again and snapped the lock on his black leather bag. "I'll have an oxygen tank sent around, and I'll see if Cora can come over and look after her." He raised his hand when Kate started to speak. "No, I don't want you doing it." He turned to Jason. "I don't want her doing it," he repeated sternly.

Jason nodded agreement and shrugged in the same motion, clearly indicating the folly of directing the stream to flow uphill, the sun not to shine in August or his wife to do other than what she had set her mind to.

"Cora's a fine nurse," Billy continued earnestly; then he paused, his hand on the doorknob. "I'm sorry, Kate. I'm awfully sorry! I could move her to the hospital in Martinsville, I could hook 'er up and plug 'er in—keep 'er alive, but she wouldn't call it that, she wouldn't want any part of it."

By late evening, the convulsions were fifteen minutes apart. Kate watched them come and go in stunned silence, unable to move from her chair at the foot of the bed, or look away. She had seen it before, but never like this, never this way. Her grandfather had taken to his bed with self-diagnosed summer croup and a few hours later had complained that his feet were cold. "Get me the afghan, Sister," and when she'd returned he'd had no need of it. Eight years later, Gran, still taut with energy, rope-veined from work, had died in her sleep after putting up eighteen quarts of peaches the day before. The grandparents had gone quietly, with no fuss, and had left behind them the gift of their own firm belief that they went surely and swiftly into the arms of a waiting Savior. Not like this. Not like this long, dark night that opened the heavy door to love's narrowest corridor, bordered on one side by resentment and on the other by guilt. And there was no Savior waiting at the end of it.

Elizabeth Warwick struggled. Her eyes rolled upward, the eyelids fluttered, the eyes rolled down again; her legs jerked under the quilt in a sad robot dance; her hands clutched at empty air, then flitted—fingers widespread as if they could not bear to touch each other—like butterflies across her chest; spit trickled from loose lips and dried in a fine white line. At the end, each time, the back arched, straining upward, and a long, shuddering breath pushed into the air, as if trying to get out, trying to escape from a treasonous body that would not even control its waste.

Cora Atherton had washed most of death's many faces, had cleaned its relaxed orifices. For her, the contorted form beneath the patchwork quilt was no outrage of twists and spasms and failing systems, but simply another poor soul to be escorted with cool cloths and warm words into the next world, or perhaps persuaded to linger awhile in this one. The Lord's will be done. Blessed is the name of the Lord. Amen.

". . . Now, now, dear, that's better . . . Let's just wipe your poor face . . . There, there . . . that's a dear girl . . ."

"Do you—do you think she's in pain?" Kate asked haltingly.

Cora smoothed the pillowslip and tucked in the sheet. "No—no," she answered, shaking her head. "She's in a deep sleep, a very deep sleep."

"But you keep talking to her—touching her."

Cora nodded. "I do that. . ." She paused, then went on apologetically, ". . . with the very sick ones. I fancy they hear the sound of my words, know someone's with them, know they're not alone."

Kate shivered. "I see. . ."

"When Mr. Barrett had his coronary, his second one, I thought sure he was a goner. He told me afterwards that he'd heard me, didn't know what I was saying, but that it was a comforting presence. He said it made him feel better

about the whole business. Whether he was going or staying, he felt better about it."

Kate took a deep breath. "I see," she repeated. "I think I
can do it—what you're doing. You must be tired and hungry. There's turkey in the refrigerator."

Cora consulted the pocket watch pinned to her starched
white bosom. "My, it is getting on. You're sure?"

"Oh yes," Kate said firmly, "I'll be fine."

Cora smoothed the pillow again, hesitated, then smiled
encouragement and left the room. Slowly, Kate approached
the bed, knelt by the side of it and took her mother's hand.
It was dry and brittle-veined like a maple leaf in late fall,
and it had a faint metallic scent—unplaceable, unpleasant.
The long polished nails were a cruel joke on such a hand; if
she held it too tightly, it would crumble into flat yellow
powder, leaving only the bright-red ovals behind.

"It's all right, Momma, it's all right . . . it's all right. . ."

The daughter's low murmurs and the mother's ragged
breathing covered the soft sound of Jason entering the
room. "Billy left orders," he said quietly, coming up behind
her.

"But she's got to know it's all right."

"What's all right, Kate?" He sank down on his haunches
next to her, his elbows resting on his knees, the fingers of
his large hands interlaced. "What do you want her to
know?" he repeated.

"That I understand why she went away—why she left us
when we were little."

"Do you?"

"No, not really. But I want her to know that I forgive
her."

Jason stood up and backed away, impatient with the hint
of piety that flavored his wife's words. "Your forgiveness,"
he said evenly, "is it such a precious thing that you've got to
bother her with it now?"

Kate stiffened and turned toward him, but before she
could speak, it started again. The clatter of breathing eased,
eyelids fluttered, and the terrible ritual began. Clumsily
and with studied effort, Kate performed the tasks she had

watched Cora accomplish with such ease, waving Jason away when he moved forward to help. She took the hand that clawed the air, plumped the pillow under the arched neck, adjusted the suction tube, and, when it was over, smoothed the hair back from the damp forehead, tucked in the sheet. As she dipped the washcloth into the basin of water on the nightstand and wrung it dry, she realized with a start that this was the first time she had ever seen her mother with an unmade face.

Cora's rubber-soled footsteps squeaked on the heavily waxed floor. She smiled professionally from behind her half-rimmed spectacles and took Elizabeth's wrist between her thumb and plump pink fingers. "Rest now," she said to Kate, "you and the mister. Poor thing, you look all tuckered out." She motioned with her free hand toward the door. "I'll call you if she takes a turn."

The kitchen was warmed by the great stone fireplace Gran Warwick had used for cooking in the early days. The appearance of the room had changed little since that time. An electric range was disguised as a turn-of-the-century coal stove. Two refrigerators were set out of view in recesses in the wall; a large freezer was hidden behind retractable wormy-chestnut paneling. An old pitcher-spout pump had been sunk into the butcher board that covered the sink counter, and pumped pure ice water from the original well. A Peerless scale in gleaming brass hung above it, and next to the scales a large pair of ice tongs. A five-gallon barrel churn was still capable of producing butter, and on holidays it did.

A solid oak table with lion-claw feet, and an assortment of oak chairs with hand-carved backs and turned spindles had come all the way from North Carolina before the Great Oklahoma Run. The table—deeply gouged by its journey, scorched by hot pots and bread pans, painted and crayoned by a series of young artists—had received the blessing of time's patina, which blended its accidents into its grain. The floor, oak-plank and punctuated here and there with hand-hooked rugs, reflected the light from the fire in its polished surface. Above it all, Gran's Sheffield pewter and Haviland graced the high mantel. It was a room which, like its mistress, carefully concealed signs of change.

Kate poured coffee, then sat stiffly in a rocker facing her husband, staring at him as if to draw his attention. "It was you, wasn't it, Jason?" she said finally.

"It was me, what?"

"You've been giving her the whiskey."

"So that's what you're so bent out of shape about." Then he nodded yes and stretched his long legs out in front of him.

"Where is it? Ever since she came home this time I've been trying to find out where she hides it."

"Hodge kept it for her. In his scout canteens."

Kate flushed and rocked furiously. "It wasn't good for her, you know. It's bad for her heart, not to mention her liver. And worse, you've taught our son to be deceitful."

Jason leaned forward, the firelight throwing warm shadows on his face. "Your mother is a grown-up woman," he said slowly. "Her internal organs are her own business. Anyway, I got tired of watching it. Her turning into some kind of barn drinker and you into some kind of Carrie Nation." Then he smiled and ducked his head in an appeal. "And please don't mention it to Hodge. I told him it would only worry you if you knew. The deceit, as you call it, is mine."

Kate sighed and looked at him, holding his gaze, waiting for something more. But his words and the smile, boyish and questioning, was as close as he would come to an apology. She knew that. She let her body go limp and stopped the chair's angry rocking.

"I called Pepper," he went on. "She'll be home tomorrow morning."

Kate nodded with relief. At worst, the household fell into a kind of holiday disorder during Pepper's occasional absences to visit her son in Washington or her sister in Louisiana, but Kate had no wish to live through the coming days without the old woman's sure and solid presence.

"And Susannah," he added. "She'll get in on Sunday."

Kate frowned. "Susannah's coming?"

His eyes widened in surprise. "Of course she's coming. She wants you to call her when you can. She's got some man she wants to bring with her—wants to know if it's okay."

"And if it isn't?" Kate said wryly. "Would that make any difference?"

"She was upset."

"Did you tell her . . .? Did you tell her Momma's. . .?"

"I told her that her mother is dying," he said gently.

Kate covered her mouth and cheeks, and spoke haltingly through her fingers. "It's true, isn't it? It's *true*. Momma's dying and there's nothing we can do for her."

Jason shifted his weight uneasily. "You could call a priest for her."

"A priest? In Grampa's house?"

"It's our house, Kate. You and I make the life-and-death decisions here."

"But I don't know if she's entitled to a priest," Kate argued lamely.

"Entitled?" Jason finished his coffee and stood up. He crossed over to Kate, leaned down and took her chin in his hand. "Think about it," he said wearily. "It's her death, not Gideon's, not yours. And they've got words for all the sheep—especially the lost and strayed ones."

Kate phoned Father Flesher in Martinsville. Yes, he understood. Yes, of course he would come. Yes, he most certainly would come right away.

In the first gray light of dawn, Elizabeth Sullivan Warwick—absolved of sin, assured the beatific vision and the soul's union with God—began to breath easily, quietly, and then not at all. It was over. A life filled with notions of what she would do tomorrow, next week, next season. Next September she would go back and finish nurse's training. Next spring she would remember to plant the Iceland poppies, and she would bring her canvases down from the attic and get some new paints. Next time she came home she would bring red lipsticks and high-heel shoes, and, what's more, she'd persuade Grampa to let the girls wear them. Next summer they really would take that trip to California. Next time she'd take up with a better sort of man. And, oh yes, next time she certainly would not drink so much, maybe even take the cure. Now, at long last, she had finished a thing she had started.

TWO

Marylouise Wright—who, in addition to raising
blood horses, contributed regularly to the *Robina Herald*'s "Poet's Corner" and "Society Scene"—wrote Elizabeth Warwick's obituary. She called the snow that came
that day "a soft, gentle benediction that clung to bare winter limbs and shingled rooftops in a stilled white world. . ."

She went on to note that Susannah Warwick, "known
professionally to her myriad admirers as Susannah Sullivan," had canceled a speaking engagement in Baltimore,
Maryland, to be with her sister for their mother's last rites.
Indeed, there was considerably more space devoted to the
live daughters than to the dead mother, but then Kate was
the town's leading citizen, and Susannah its celebrity—the
only one the small community had enjoyed since a retired
federal marshal settled there in 1910.

Susannah was, according to *Time*, "a feisty lady with a
cause for all seasons." At her best, she wrote and spoke
with evocative eloquence and informed clarity on sexual
freedom, birth control, equal wages for equal work, and
woman's inalienable right to explore her vast potential. At
her worst, she was simply and deliberately outrageous, em-

bracing whatever current issue had shock value in the marketplace, and in this light (or rather heat) was a natural for late-night talk shows.

Robina, Oklahoma, conservative both politically and morally, heartily disapproved of Susannah, but had by silent assent agreed that fame had its privileges, among them eccentricity. Besides, she was Gideon Warwick's granddaughter and, as his legacy, would always be welcome. Please let it be briefly and in small discreet doses.

Kate too had enjoyed her share of publicity, albeit local, her activities diligently followed by the *Herald* during the thirty-five years after it had announced her birth: "*cum laude* graduate of Oklahoma A and M;" "comely and radiant in Irish lace over slipper satin;" "new president of the PTA;" "district representative to the Regional Teachers' Meeting in Kansas City;" "energetic mother of four;" and "doing nicely after a broken arm suffered last Thursday in a fall off of old Charlie."

The sisters were born in a flurry of maternity thirteen months apart, both cut from the same fair and sturdy Scots-Irish cloth, but Susannah, the younger, stitched up like a Saturday-night party dress. Their father, Adam Warwick, was kicked to death breaking a horse when the girls were three and two, and their mother (as was noted in the *Herald* obituary) left Robina soon after the tragedy to go into nurse's training in Oklahoma City. The grandparents then raised them as they had their father before them, in a black-and-white world as predictable as lady apples in December. They were children of the Great Depression, but it touched them not at all. While the country struggled to its feet, Gideon Warwick resisted hail, drought, grasshoppers and the Agricultural Adjustment Act in order to farm his twelve hundred acres as he saw fit, run between a hundred fifty and two hundred head of beef cattle, and earn a reputation for wisdom and strength that made him a legend throughout Robina County. As with all legends, time dimmed much of the truth of Gideon, so that it became more and more difficult to separate the myth from the man.

"'Member the time Gideon run the government man off his place with a shotgun?" one of the old men would say.

"And when he told Edwards to go ahead and take that Jew's money, then hide them pigs in the holler?" another would chortle, slapping his knee.

Caught up and carried away into the past, the old men would sit rocking on their porches, pulling on their pipes, reliving events that never took place. Gideon never lifted a gun in anger, and what he told Matthew Edwards went more like "We can make it, Matt. We can make it together. Plant your upper field in potatoes and half the cornfield in vegetables. Trade some of your pigs to me for beef, some to Tom for sheep and smoke, and can what you can't feed. We can ride this thing out if we all work together."

It was not that he didn't respect the United States government and her problem of overproduction and underconsumption. He did. He held his country in profound reverence. But the prospect of plowing under God's bounty and slaughtering God's beasts for other than food seemed to him an unnatural, wasteful and blasphemous solution. Thus Gideon Warwick, holding firm to his belief that prosperity was invented by the Republican Party, nevertheless created for himself and his neighbors a small island of socialism, damning that dreamer Henry Wallace every step of the way.

The addition of two small girl children to the circle of his responsibility presented no problem for Gideon or for Gran either. The old virtues were required of them, that was all; that they be honest, hardworking and chaste; that they fear God, do justly and love mercy, honor their elders and feed and water their animals before they themselves sat down to supper.

Death spared him a changing world, one where his black and white standards were questioned, mocked, and even legislated against. But Gideon's faith was sown deep in the issue of his own house. Without cultivation, without tending, his spirit would sprout and bloom in mysterious and unexpected ways.

THREE

SUSANNAH WAS out of her seat belt and into her full-
length sable coat before the wheels hit the runway of the
Tulsa airport. She spoke in a distracted and abrupt way to
the man next to her. "You get the bags, huh, Marty? And
I'll rent us a car."

"Okay if I wait till the plane lands, your ladyship?"

She smiled sheepishly. "Quite all right, my good man.
And while you're at it, will you see if you can find my ruby
slippers. I may need them."

He grinned, showing white even teeth, and settled back
for the landing. Marty Stone had, off and on for twelve
years, picked up the bags for Susannah. As her agent, her
friend, her sometimes lover—though long since not in passion—he had watched her acquire the tools for success, the
weapons for survival; had observed the process from its
very beginning when she stood opposite his desk, virginal,
Ivory-scrubbed and smelling faintly of lavender, clutching
her white gloves in her hand, stubbornly insisting that she
was *not* just another escaped Homecoming Queen.

The stewardess paused and smiled down at Marty as she
moved along collecting the last of the empty cups. He

smiled back, acknowledging the compliment, returning it in kind, stating clearly in a silent, ancient language that yes it would be nice but you see this dance is taken. Another time, another place, another flight. He turned his head and followed her progress down the aisle, knowing from the slow easy swing of her hips (which were also very nice) that she knew he watched her. And as the old saying went, that she knew that he knew that she knew . . . The smiles from the pretty ladies had always been welcome, but never so much as now. Now that he clung by an elastic thread to forty, often longing for the grace of the ass-end of middle age when he wouldn't worry about the twenty extra pounds, then repenting and scheduling four sets of tennis back to back to get into fighting trim or sailing trim or, let's face it, fucking trim. Nothing took the fun out of it quicker than too much belly on the leading edge. But he never missed Sundays. Every Sunday morning he took off a good three pounds playing polo at the Will Rogers estate. He had started to play because it seemed to lend him an air of respectability—a rich man's sport, old and honored. He had kept it up because he liked it, even if the three pounds were instantly reinstated with blueberry blintzes at the Polo Lounge. The face was changing, too: a little bleariness in the blue-white whites of his eyes; a little extra flesh along the chin line; a little less fine black hair on the hairline. Teeth still very good, though, thanks to compulsive habits and modern dentistry.

It was said of Marty Stone—sometimes kindly—that he had more fading female clients over forty than any other agent in town. It was not generally appreciated that because he too had been beautiful he understood the importance of the loss.

Twenty-one years before, while shaving, he had divined, in one of those clear and sudden flashes of understanding, that his face, with just a small assist from the rest of him, could earn him a fortune. The next day he dropped out of NYU, where he was a failing drama major, and hitchhiked to Hollywood to become a movie star. Not an actor—a movie star. He made that distinction in his mind. But soon after he got there he took a long look at the odds—odds being something for which he had an intuitive, gut feeling—and with not even a twinge of regret amended his plans for the future.

Marty was, in the best sense of the word, a hustler, hustling not people but circumstances. And he had an unfailing eye for what was called star quality. Within two years after his arrival at Sunset and Highland in the back of an old Ford pickup, he was representing a small but heavy-duty list of clients and was clearly on the way up.

Two years later, on an otherwise ordinary Sunday afternoon, and without stopping to compute the percentages, survey the probabilities or figure the odds, he fell in love, and this act of faith changed for him the shape and the rotation and the meaning of the world.

Two years after that, she died giving birth to their child. The baby—a girl, five pounds and jaundiced—lived in a feeble, heartbreaking way for another four days. He took them back to San Antonio to his wife's parents to be buried, and after the funeral he went on a year-long binge.

One morning he woke up in a motel in Fresno with no memory of how or when he had got there. No memory, either, of the assortment of spaced-out naked bodies that littered the room. He got up and, in the bluish light of the stark-white bathroom, brought the odds up close to his sore yellow eyes so he could get a good look at them. He showered, got dressed, forgave himself and the fates for his incompatible blood type as best he could, and went back to work.

The engines roared. The plane taxied up the runway. Marty looked past Susannah, through the small pane and into the snow-banked loading area. "Make sure that car's got chains," he said. She nodded, her face pale and expressionless. He patted her hand, and she turned to face him. "You okay, hon?" he asked.

"Yeah, I'm okay."

"Listen, I know it's hard—losing people, family. If you want to talk about it—"

"That's not it, Marty," she interrupted. "I have a lot of less than sparkling qualities, but hypocrisy is not one of them. Momma's been dead and buried for a long time. She didn't bother about me, I didn't bother about her. Even trade."

"You use her name. You must have—"

"Euphonious reasons, not affectionate ones."

Marty frowned. "Come on, Susannah, don't be an asshole."

She lifted her eyebrows in innocent archs. "I'm not being an asshole, I'm being honest."

"Well, then," he said, "please be honest quietly. Some of my cells are dying."

"That's a nonsequitur."

"It's my defense against wrongheadedness."

She sighed. "What I meant is that this is just a formality."

"*Fin*ality," he said by way of correction. "There's a big difference."

"Oh, I suppose so." She smiled and put her cheek next to his. "Hey! I really appreciate your coming with me, I really do! I know you have other things to do besides hand-holding, but I sure am glad you're here."

The engines shut off abruptly, and she reached under the seat for her train case. When she lifted her head there were deep toothmarks in her lower lip. "Just once," she said angrily, "just *once*, I'd like to come back here feeling welcome!"

Fifteen minutes out of the rental-car parking lot, they turned off the main highway onto a two-lane blacktop road that twisted and curved over one-lane bridges and humpy culverts. The fields on either side—a richness of corn, wheat, barley and alfalfa in the spring—joined the sky in winter's unending barrenness, interrupted by stark barbed-wire fences and lonely gray farmhouses. Along the way, sad-faced red-and-white Herefords brought color to the landscape as they huddled together for warmth with short-legged black Angus.

"They die sometimes when they do that," Susannah said absently. "They don't freeze—you'd think they'd freeze like coots freeze at the edge of pond ice, but they don't. They smother each other getting too close. Ironic, isn't it?"

"Ummmm," Marty grunted, intent on the road ahead.

"Kate and Jason raise Sanlanders," she began again, then stopped. "You want to hear this? Am I bothering you? I know I'm just nattering on, but I guess I'm nervous."

"No, go ahead. I'm interested."

"He started out—Jason, I mean—with Santa Gertrudis. That's a cross between a shorthorn and a Brahman. He crossed them with Highlanders to get a breed better suited to this climate and to cut down on cake feeding. The Highlander's very hearty, does well on poor pasture, and the Santa Gertrudis is a big gainer—"

"You really know this shit, don't you?"

She shrugged. "I guess so. I grew up with it. Grampa was a cattleman—not like Jason, of course, but I guess there's the residue. Like the language. Every time I'm here, in spite of all those expensive talking lessons, right away I'm drawling and twanging through my nose and using words I thought I'd long forgotten." She laughed. "I guess we never really get shed of our native tongue."

Marty brought the car to a snow-crunch stop. The sign to the right said this was Robina, population 1245, and a Garden Club City. The one on the left offered Eats, Gas, and Clean Rest Rooms.

"We turn right at the railroad crossing, on up a little ways."

"Where's Robina?"

"To the left and around the bend: a bank, two general stores, a harness shop, garage, drugstore, post office, one abandoned hotel, the Community House and nine churches."

Marty laughed. "You're putting me on. A town with only twelve hundred potential souls to save has got nine churches? How can it support that many?"

"Easy. The members of the congregation build the church, then when it starts to look rundown at the heels they get together and give it a fresh coat of paint, hammer a few nails, say a few hallelujahs, and have a potluck supper. Most of the ministers are full-time farmers, they're not ordained or anything like that, they just have the calling. The pay is the jollies they get leading the flock into terminal righteousness, and a calf or a pig or some such for weddings and funerals. Just like in the old days."

"Did you go to one of them?"

"You damn betcha. The Beulah Baptist Church of Robina, Sunday morning, Sunday evening, and Wednesday Night Prayer Meeting till I was sixteen years old."

"Then you started to backslide?"

"No." Susannah laughed, then shook her head back and forth and said in slow measured words, "The new preacher offended my granddaddy's sense of propriety. He delivered a hellfire-and-damnation sermon about how the Jews killed Christ—no mention, of course, of any assistance from the Romans—and that they would be forever responsible, generation unto generation. Grampa just wasn't having any part of that kind of yellow journalism." She laughed again with the pleasure of the recollection. "Right in the middle of the service, he gathers up Gran and Kate and Pepper and me and off we go, shirttails flapping in the breeze, down the road to the Methodists."

"Pepper? Pepper?" Marty said, looking puzzled. "Ah yes, I remember—the old family retainer."

"And cook and conscience and resident wise old bird," Susannah added fondly. Then she turned and looked at Marty for a long moment. "About that other," she said hesitantly, "I know it sounds archaic, but some of these good Christian folk may look on you as an oddity."

He smiled. "They don't go in for tar and feathering, do they? Or cross burning?"

"No, of course not. As a matter of fact, they're very good people, hardworking, salt-of-the-earth, shirt-off-your-back, last-dime folks. It's just that, well, most of them have never seen a real live Jew. They'll expect you to fit the clichés. You'll catch somebody looking at you sideways trying to locate where you keep your horns, and sure as anything somebody'll say something about being jewed down on a corn crop. I just don't want you to be uncomfortable."

Marty waved his unconcern. "Hey! We all do some of that. I'd never seen a real live Okie before I met you. I thought you were all barefoot and illiterate."

Susannah grinned, settled into her coat, pushed her feet closer to the heater, and leaned her head on the back of the seat. Animated or in repose as it was now, her face missed classical description by a nose that was too small and slightly off center. But not off center enough to make the face distinctive. She was frequently, maddeningly, mistaken for someone's sister from Des Moines—or "Didn't we go to high school together in St. Louis?" Or: "Isn't it amazing! Henry, it is absolutely *amazing!* She looks exactly like your cousin Christine. My goodness, yes. Same hair, same way of talking, same eyes. Well, come to think of it, there's a difference in the eyes. . ."

People remembered the eyes: winter-ocean gray with astonishing dark rings around the edge of the iris—clear, bright with the alertness of a devout listener. Her pale-blond hair was a remarkable Clairol copy of the shade it had been until it started to darken—despite desperate doses of summer sun and lemon juice—in her last year of high school. Now, as then, she brushed it back from its widow's peak and let it settle on its own around her face, on her shoulders—the difference being the cost of the hairdresser to keep it looking as if it required no effort. Susannah was not beautiful and was satisfied, for the most part, to be what she was: ripe-looking and lushly pretty in a wind-blown way; and mildly resentful that it was taking more and more time, energy, restraint, and money to remain that way.

"What are those?" Marty asked suddenly.

"Ummmm?" Susannah blinked and yawned.

"The humps in the ground. I've seen them all along the way. With the poles sticking up out of them?"

"Storm cellars. Pepper calls them fruit caves. You are smack-dab in the middle of tornado country, my good man.

Sometimes in the spring we'd spend more nights in the cellar than we did in our own beds."

"In the spring, huh? That's good, we're early."

"Oh, don't worry. There hasn't been a tornado here since nineteen ought seven. My grandfather's ghost protects Robina County. He went out to meet the last one that tried to come through and parted the wind like Moses at the Red Sea."

Marty laughed. "Susannah, you are so full of it."

"I'm just telling you the local lore. You can go into town on any April day and the old men sitting on the hotel steps will give you the straight poop. A cyclone came out of the east, and Gideon met it in the fields. He straddled the crops and shook his fist and said this was sacred ground—that he had a covenant with the Lord, and the wind was to move on its way."

"You're not laughing."

"No," she said thoughtfully. "I guess I believe it. Oh, look," she said suddenly, and pointed to the side of the road. "It starts here." Barbed-wire fencing gave way to neat white rail. "All Kate's," she said, barely above a whisper. "Six sections; six hundred and forty acres to a section; both sides of the road as far as the eye can see. Grampa left her this on the right and she married this on the left."

Marty inclined his head toward her, keeping his eyes on the road. "I'm sorry, hon, I didn't hear you."

"It's nothing," she said, shrugging it off, then added, again in a whisper, "Only the heart of the matter."

"Susannah, you'll have to speak up—"

"Turn in up there where the gate's open," she interrupted, and moments later they rattled over the cattle guard. She leaned forward expectantly. "You can see the house over the next rise."

It stood in a grove of pecan trees: white frame, two-story, with a lattice-enclosed porch that completely encircled the house. Two gables and a turret gave it a haunted, Victorian look, quickly dispelled by the warm welcome of a grass-green swing and wicker chairs. Behind and to the right a new stable and a paddock had been added, and the old smokehouse torn down. Everything else was the same: the red barns and outbuildings straight out of a child's picture book: the dogs, dutifully announcing the arrival of visitors, then running back to warm beds under the house.

Marty brought the car to a stop, switched off the ignition and turned to Susannah. "Well. . .?"

"Well. . .?" she echoed, then let out a long despairing breath. "Remember that thing about the hired man?" And, without waiting for him to remember, said, "Home is the place where, when you have to go there, they have to take you in."

FOUR

THROUGH THE slightly parted lace curtains at the kitchen window, Kate watched them get out of the car. The man grinned, reached down for a handful of snow, and molded it lightly between his gloved hands. Susannah laughed and ducked down out of sight, then moments later raised up slowly, waving a white handkerchief. The man pulled a disappointed face, dropped the snowball, then went around and opened the trunk. Susannah was gesturing and pointing like some sort of tour guide as he handed her a train case and a wardrobe bag. She took them, then tossed her head, her hair gleaming as it floated above the deep-brown fur of her coat. The breath of their words, their laughter, rolled into the air.

Unconsciously, Kate's hands went to her own hair, smoothed it back into its neat chestnut chignon, then pulled wisps from behind her ears, twisted them around her fingers and coaxed them forward. She looked down at the beige silk shirtwaist that had seemed so elegant when she put it on an hour ago and now was so drab and matronly. Her sister had always had that effect on her, and it didn't help, never had helped, that she knew, objectively, she was just as attractive in her own pale, delicate way, with the same oval, finely structured face, the same striking gray eyes spaced far apart beneath a high smooth forehead, the same silken hair—an impartial gift from their mother. She suffered from the comparisons she herself seemed compelled to note: the difference in the length of dark lashes, in the high firmness of unnursed breasts, in the sensual pouting fullness of the lower lip, and in the abiding grace of confidence.

Confidence that came, Kate was certain, from early expression of unconditional love. And because she had worn the same shoe on both feet, she also knew that love was dished up unequally like strawberries, and that often the larger, sweeter portion went to those who took it as their due, not to those who stood back and reflected on the disparity. But it didn't help to be able to name one's own devils. It never had helped.

They started toward the house, Susannah doing a playful half-skip, kicking snow in front of her, still laughing, the man following with luggage. When she was a girl, Kate had watched this same scene from this same window so many times: her mother laughing, hurrying toward the house; a man, always different from the last one, following with her bags, depositing them on the front porch, waving his promise to come back for her on Sunday evening or the end of the week or—on rare occasions—the end of the month.

But this wasn't Momma. Momma lay in an overheated, overflowered room in the Whittaker Funeral Home in Martinsville, as restless in death as she had been in life. First the trip to the hospital for what was surely an unnecessary autopsy; then to the funeral home, downstairs to be prepared, upstairs to be visited. Monday she would come back to Robina for services in the Community House, then finally return to the outskirts of Martinsville, to The Meadows, to lie with her husband Adam, and Gideon and Gran.

Requiescant in pace.

No, this was not Momma. This was Susannah, the silver sibling, the golden girl, the favored one, lifting her chin as

if to be photographed, reaching out her eager, slender-fin-
gered hands for the big dish of strawberries . . .

"She's here!" Page shouted, clattering down the stairs
two at a time. "Susannah's here!"

"*Aunt* Susannah," Kate corrected him.

He raced to the door and flung it open. "Susannah!"

She stopped short, dropped the bags in the snow, then
rushed up the porch steps, where she made a slow, wondering circle around him. "Can this be Page? I don't believe it!
Is it really you? So tall and handsome and grown up?"

He flushed with pleasure. "I saw you on TV last month.
Boy, you were neat." He glanced toward the doorway and
lowered his voice to a conspiratorial whisper. "Really
bitchin'."

She flashed Marty a how-about-that look, then said,
"Why, thank you, Page—I think." Then she looked past
him to where her sister stood in the open door, and her
breath, her laughter caught in her throat. As she gazed into
Kate's smooth, milk-white, unadorned face, she felt a zit
begin to gather and bloom on the side of her nose, though
she'd not had that problem since adolescence and then—so
said her clear-faced sister—because she had fleshy thoughts.
Her skin felt heavy with makeup, she was glossy and over-
dressed, her hair was too long, too blond. She glanced down
at her feet and saw, instead of the smart Italian boots, penny
moccasins that wanted polish. She was cut too low all over,
and had lint in the dusty corners of her untidy life.

Kate stretched out her arms and noticed that her hands
trembled. She stopped short. "Welcome home, Susannah."

Susannah held out her own hands from where she stood,
and they clasped each other by their fingertips. Neither
could be sure of who held whom at arm's length.

Inside, children appeared out of nowhere, all talking and
laughing at once. Marty was introduced and then ignored
in the confusion that followed. Susannah was unusually
successful, even for a childless, absentee aunt. She had
never forgotten a birthday, a holiday, and she always sent
the gifts parents never provided because they were too

quixotic or too extravagant. She had a special knack for remembering those things treasured, for searching out and identifying those things special.

Now she called up for each child an event shared when she was there last, and made each one seem like a talisman she had carried with her. "How's your bird-calling, Meg?" And the pink, dimpled five-year-old clapped her hands and brought them under her chin, remembering how the finch had cocked its head and fluttered its wings in response to the sounds she had made. She lifted her arms to be picked up and demanded they go find cardinals to feed that very moment. Patrick, shy and short on words at seven, was encouraged to talk at length about every board and nail he had used in the construction of his tree house. Behind Patrick stood Hodge, in startling contrast to the blue-eyed fairness of the others, lithe and brown as a young brave, his eyes so dark it was not possible to discern where the pupil stopped and the iris began. At eleven, he had conquered the world of childhood and hovered over an early adolescence, not quite willing to shut the door on the years he had mastered. He could run faster, climb higher, swim farther, and collect smoother, flatter rocks for pond-skipping than any other boy in Robina County.

It was Hodge who had greeted her the last time. It was not a death that had brought her, but rather she had made a pilgrimage. The divorce from Blair, her second marital failure in five years, had left her feeling orphaned and betrayed and had sent her to Robina in search of a feeling of family.

He had walked toward the car with the slow, solemn steps of an old man, barefoot and shirtless in the late Oklahoma spring, his jeans cut off above the knee.

She had smiled, not sure which one of her sister's large litter this would be.

Hi, he had said, shoving his hands into his back pockets.

She inclined her head and looked him up and down. Let's see, now. With all that dark hair you must be Hodge?

Yes, ma'am. He returned her scrutiny. You must be Susannah.

She nodded and pursed her lips. You certainly have grown!

I'm nine now. He spoke instructively, patiently, as if explaining this phenomenon of growth that adults had such difficulty comprehending. I was five when you came before. He moved his hands from his back pockets to the front and then folded them across his chest. He opened his mouth to speak and then closed it, ducking his head, burrowing a toe into the dirt.

What is it? she asked.

There's some bad news and I thought I should be the one that's to tell it. He spoke defensively, as if angry with her for this task she necessitated. She waited quietly, her eyes encouraging him to go on. He breathed deeply with a false start, then plunged in. It's about Bright Feather. She got something wrong inside, a twisted intestine, Jason figured. We tried to make her well, even had a vet down from Tulsa, but he couldn't do anything either. Jason went ahead and doctored her for a time, but she just got worse. He bit his lip and turned his head away. I hate to give you bad news when you first come, but I thought you'd want to get it over with. I always like to get bad news over with . . . He searched her face and breathed his relief when she told him that she was sure they had done all they could.

She was mine, he continued. I know she belonged to you, but she was mine to take care of. I have her foal—a mare. He added shyly, I named her The Sullivan. That's for you and Gramma.

I take that kindly, Susannah said, and the phrase, long unused, felt strange on her tongue.

Jason cried when he had to shoot her, but he wouldn't ask any of the hands to do it. We were afraid you might not like it that we didn't ask you, but she got worse all of a sudden and Pepper said you wouldn't want her hurting.

She nodded. Did you? Did you cry?

No. Yes, but it's just between him and me. Pepper says

it's sinful to waste tears on animals when so many two-footed creatures are in need of them.

Oh, bother Pepper, Susannah smiled. I expect we have enough tears to go around. She opened the car door, and then, as if she had just heard him speak, as if it had just registered, said, Jason? You call him Jason?

Hodge nodded that he did. I have for a long time, he said. Since I was little. It isn't meant disrespectful . . .

"Do you get to ride out in California?" the older, taller Hodge asked now, having waited his turn, having listened with filial discomfort while Page, with all the subtlety of a cow chip in the milk bucket, tried to wangle a summer invitation to Disneyland.

Susannah sighed regretfully. "Not anymore, no time. But Marty does, he plays polo. I bet he'd enjoy riding Western."

"Would you, sir?"

"It's no fun riding in the snow," Page said quickly, interrupting Marty's affirmative answer.

"It's not snowing now, and it's not deep."

"The drifts are deep."

"What's polo?" asked Meg.

"We're not going to ride in the *drifts*," Hodge said impatiently. Then to his sister, "It's kind of like a game of hockey on horseback, Meggie."

"Well, it's not good for the horses. They don't think it's fun," Page persisted.

"Polo?"

"No, Meggie, the snow."

The argument was interrupted by sounds of feet stamping and scrapping on the front porch. The door opened and Jason came in, smiling and blowing on his hands. "Welcome home, stranger," he said, bobbing his head toward Susannah. The smile faded and he took off his hat, holding it awkwardly in front of him. "I'm sorry about the circumstances."

Susannah nodded and spoke in an oddly formal tone. "Thank you, Jason, I'm sorry, too."

He cocked his head and narrowed his eyes. "How long's it been now?"

"Two years," she said shortly. "But you were off somewhere buying cattle, or selling them. Six. It's been six years in June since Gran died." She was silent a moment, then, "Oh!"—flustered—"I'm sorry. This is Marty—my agent, Marty Stone."

The two men shook hands, performed the rituals of I'm-pleased-to and I'm-glad-to, then both stepped back into place, Jason shifting uneasily from one foot to the other, Marty reflecting on the charged air that seemed to fill the room.

"Marty does polo," said Meg brightly. "It's like hockey on horses."

"Is that a fact?" Jason said, looking either astonished or appalled, Marty wasn't sure which.

"Just a hobby I fell into," Marty said quickly. "It sweats off a few pounds," he added in an offhand way, wondering why he suddenly felt a need to apologize for risking life and limb every Sunday.

"Hummm." Jason Garrity was, of course, incapable of rudeness to a guest in his own house, but he was equally incapable of expressing enthusiasm for any kind of exercise where a man had to get himself up in fancy gear. There was plenty of sweat to be shed in hard work. But then, if you earned your bread on other folks' labors . . . Nonetheless, he roused himself to graciousness. "You may want to have a go at one of our Arabs. We could probably get the loan of an English saddle from Marylouise, don't you think so, Kate?"

"I think I can manage to stay up in the Western variety," Marty said smoothly.

"Well, whichever—first you need to get settled," Kate interrupted.

Susannah craned her neck toward the door to the kitchen. "Where's Pepper?"

"She went into town to pick up some more groceries. So many people have come by to pay their respects, you know—she'll be back directly—of course she's beside herself—can't wait to see her 'darlin' baby'." Kate laughed nervously; she was like a small, buff-colored bird, flitting from subject to subject. "I've put you in our old room, and Mr. Stone—" She turned to Marty. "May I call you Marty?" He said he would like that, and she added in a curiously shy tone, "And you will call me Kate. You're in the sunroom—it's the very nicest room in the house. There'll be people again this afternoon, and Father Flesher is coming—" Her words fell over one another as if hoping to go unnoticed. "We'll put out a buffet and—"

"Father who?"

"I'll tell you all about it while you unpack. Hodge, please show Marty to his room, and don't badger him with questions about California. He'd probably like to shower and change. Hear?"

There was a general dispersal, and Kate's mind rushed ahead of her up the staircase to the jonquil-yellow bedroom that had been the setting for so many past confrontations; indeed, one particularly violent exchange had involved the color of the room itself, with Susannah clinging like a tick to her choice of bishop's purple. Over the years and through the spectrum, it had absorbed everything from bone-picking squabbles to roll-around brawls to days and nights of chilled silence; accusations so strident as to set the household's collective teeth on edge, about who had been so vile (one of Kate's favored denouncements at the time) as to intrude on the privacy of a diary; a continuing vendetta— still extant—arising from the question of who was truly Marylouise's very best friend; gravely innocent denials (from both of them in a rare united front) when Gran discovered the carton of Chesterfields in the hatbox on the closet shelf; and a remarkably civil conversation with respect to who told Grampa about Susannah being locked out of the dorm and violating curfew.

Finally, it was in that very room, returned two years ago to its original sunny shade of yellow, that total war had been declared over Gran's Meissen salt-and-pepper set.

Susannah moved about, draping dresses on satin-covered

hangers, carelessly folding lingerie into the violet-scented drawers, while Kate sat quietly on the bed. Watching her. Waiting.

"Did she suffer?" Susannah asked suddenly.

"Billy said she didn't. So did Cora. Cora said it was like a deep sleep. She was in the attic looking through those old pictures of us—you know, in the shoeboxes—the ones she was always going to put in an album. Remember the one of us on the Shetland pony?" Susannah nodded, smiling faintly, and Kate went on. "She had it in her hand."

"And?"

"It was an aneurysm, massive hemmorhage. There was never any hope." She blinked at the sharp sound of a drawer slammed shut.

"So now you've invited the good father to come speak about retribution overtaking the sinner?"

"It won't be that way."

"Oh? Really? You think she'll get the Twenty-third Psalm?"

"Jason said she would have wanted a priest," Kate said stiffly.

"Jason?"

"He was Momma's friend. He understood her better than any of us did." Kate's face was drawn and pale, her shoulders slumped in weariness. "Let's not argue, Susannah. Please. *This* time, let's not argue. It was our decision to make, and we did what we thought best." She smiled patiently, offering peace. "There won't be a Mass, just a simple service in the Community House."

"Ummm. You mean Momma was so blackhearted she's been denied the last sacraments?"

"No, of course not! Father Flesher gave her extreme unction. She wasn't conscious, but when there's a danger of death there doesn't have to be a confession. And he said he would say Mass if we wanted it."

A slow, knowing smile spread across Susannah's face, and she leveled a look at her sister that stopped her words. "I see," she said softly. "I got the picture. A little private forgiveness but no public display."

Kate brought her open palm to her forehead and squeezed her eyes shut. "Susannah," she cried in exasperation. "Why are you so provoking? I thought *you* would object to a Mass. You've run all over the country, popping off, talking about birth control and abortion and how the church is the enemy. I heard you say that, Susannah—to my everlasting embarrassment, I might say: right on national television you said the Catholic Church was mankind's biggest enemy. All considered, I find your attitude in this a bit hypocritical!"

Susannah waved her hand in annoyance. "That has to do with life, not death. I'm pro-abortion, I'm anti–death of the human spirit."

"You're not making sense. Abortion is death!"

"And women having kids they can't feed, can't clothe, can't educate, can't even love because they're so goddamn tired—"

"You're a real expert on that subject, aren't you?" Kate said sarcastically.

Susannah raised her arms in the air. "Wait! Halt! Cease and desist! Let's not go into my wretched state of barrenness again, okay? I give up . . . I retreat . . . I recant. Here, dear lady, is my sword. And anyway, we're off the track. We were talking about Momma—about Momma's 'simple' ceremony."

There was a long silence. Kate eyed Susannah with suspicion. When she spoke, she watched her sister with the same wary expression one gives a strange, large dog. "Father Flesher will conduct a short service, then we'll go to The Meadows for the interment, then back to the Community House. There'll be a devotional with hymns and recollections, and Marylouise will read something from *Leaves of Grass*."

Susannah flopped down on the bed opposite Kate, her eyes wide in feigned astonishment. "My God," she cried, "it's not a funeral—it's a production."

Kate was suddenly filled with overwhelming anger. It was Susannah's way to ridicule her "marvelous provincialism," to laugh heartily at traditions that were as necessary to Kate's survival as each breath she took. "You know how

it is! You know how we are! The people here expect to take
part, to pay their respects."

"To Momma? At this late date? Oh no, Sister Kate, it's
Gideon's rich granddaughter they pay their respects to; to
the local subsidy office for a dry summer or a hard winter."

"There's some of that, yes," Kate agreed. She was
thoughtful for a moment, seeming to take in the room, to
take in her sister, with all her senses. When she spoke, her
voice was dangerously low-pitched, her words raw-edged.
"You don't really care, do you? Deep down, you don't give
a damn one way or the other. If I had arranged for a Methodist service, you'd be up on your high horse about how
Momma ought to have a priest! This is all contrariness and
you know it! Your own way, that's what you want—that's
all you've ever wanted."

She paused to let the walls add this to their store. Yes,
this was much better; much better than the anxious politeness. This, then, was where they would dwell for the next
few days: on that well-kenned ground where they squared
off and let fly with poison-tipped shafts of words. At least it
was familiar.

She took a deep breath and went on. "I'm the one who's
been looking after her; I'm the one who closed her eyes. I'll
decide how she's to be buried. If you don't like it, you can
just pack up all your designer outfits and go back to California."

Susannah was silent, with downcast eyes.

Kate stood up and let out a long sigh. "I really did want
you to come, Susannah. I was unfair to you when you were
here last time, and I wanted to make it up somehow. . ."
Her words trailed off. She shrugged helplessly, unable to
rescue the dangling sentence, leaving it floating eerily in the
air as she left the room.

Susannah sat quite still. She felt a knot begin to form in
her stomach, twisting and twining in a hopeless tangle
toward that empty space where her heart should be. Why
did you do that? she asked herself accusingly. Why do you
always pick a fight with her? But she had no ready answer.

She finished unpacking, then walked aimlessly around

the room, reaching out to touch the memories that filled it. A jewelry box with the Kappa Alpha lions and shield on top—sweet Southern knights, magnolia-scented chivalry, deep, formal bows before back-seat seduction. The Pooh bear with a chewed ear, maimed foot and one blinded eye—Momma had brought stuffed animals long after they had outgrown them. The signed movie-star pictures, crinkling and yellowing, thumbtacked to the inside of the closet door. The portable record player, and albums of old 78s in alphabetical order. A collection of empty perfume bottles: Je Reviens—indeed I *have* returned—Famed Tigress, with My Sin, my White Shoulders, my bouquet of Jungle Gardenias . . .

How like Kate, not only to preserve the past but to keep it dusted.

From her train case, Susannah took a plastic bag of cosmetics, a comb, a brush, and arranged them on the chintz-skirted dressing table. There was a picture in a heavy gold frame. She had one like it, a snapshot in an album; but this one, enlarged and edged in filigreed gold, was an almost intolerable reminder. Thoughts of the day it was taken descended upon her like a band of desperados. It was—she had said so at the time—a glistening day, a day with no shadows.

As the past, like morning fog, warm and clammy, swept and swirled around her, she wondered idly why her sister had given this picture—*this of all pictures*—a place of honor; wondered if she had forgotten, or else was unable to forget, that Pepper had snapped the three of them, Kate, Susannah and Jason, in the porch swing just moments after Jason, in his new double-breasted suit, had nervously, gravely asked Gideon for Susannah's hand.

FIVE

"WELL, I think he's too old for you," Kate called to her from across the wide span, the deep col, of years.

"Twenty-five isn't old," she heard herself answer, saw herself answer between bites of hamburger.

"But these men who've been to war are used to another kind of woman."

"What other kind is there?"

"You know what I mean. With loose morals."

Susannah attacked her chocolate sundae and looked around the drugstore, crowded with lunchtime students. "I don't think foreign girls are any different than we are here," she said earnestly. "If we had bombs dropping on our heads every day, we probably wouldn't worry about saving it for a preacher and a long white dress."

"We would if we'd been raised properly," Kate answered primly, picking at her cottage-cheese salad and casting covetous eyes toward the sundae.

"Has he tried—you know—to take advantage of you?" she added in a low voice.

"Oh, Kate, for chrissake! We've known Jason all our lives. You know he's not like that."

"I've seen him put his hands on you. Right under your—ah—your bust. It's disgusting."

Susannah pointed her spoon at her sister. "Just what is it you want to know? Have I slept with him? Is that it?"

Kate flushed. "Well, you've certainly had the opportunity. It isn't decent for a nineteen-year-old girl to go to a man's apartment, and it isn't decent for a college man to *have* an apartment, for that matter."

Susannah dropped the spoon and extended both arms wide. "Oh, Kate, can't you understand? It has nothing to do with decency. We don't have orgies in his apartment. We listen to records and study and talk about life and cook spaghetti and make love—yes! make love—but it falls far short, unfortunately, of what you've got in mind.

"The truth of it is that I've done my damndest to take advantage of *him*, but he says it'd be dishonorable because of his obligations to Grampa. I haven't done any more with Jason in his apartment than I have with a half a dozen other guys in the back seat of their cars."

"I'd just as soon not hear about it," Kate snapped, returning with vigorous interest to her cottage cheese.

"Well, I'd just as soon you did! I don't know if I can explain it, if I can find the right words. It's so strange and wonderful and terrible. He walks into the room, or the drugstore, or the union, or I see him across the campus, and something happens to my body. Something really happens, Kate, something physical! My heart pounds, my stomach feels funny, my legs get weak, I get pricklies all over my skin, and I . . . I just sing all over.

"It's like getting to the top of a mountain. It's feeling and seeing and tasting things I never knew existed. When we have a fight and he doesn't call, I die—just die! Then the phone rings and it's him and I feel like crying and laughing and running in the rain and doing wild, silly things. I don't think about just sleeping with him. I think about getting up in the morning with him every day of my life and belonging to him and making breakfast for him and having his babies."

Her eyes glistened with the thought of bearing Jason's

child, and she was held spellbound by her own words. When the vision cleared, she looked blankly at Kate, as if surprised to find her still there.

She shrugged. "But that isn't what you want to hear, is it? You want to know about the other stuff—the nasty stuff."

"Keep your voice down, Susannah."

"You want to know what it's like having a man's hands on your—what did you call it? When you measure it for a pattern it's your bust, Kate, but when a man puts his hands there—" She stopped, then went on with inspired mischief, "—his mouth there, it's your breast."

Kate pushed her plate away, gathered her books from the seat beside her and scrambled, red-faced, out of the booth. "You're wicked, Susannah," she hissed. "You're vile and wicked, and God will punish you!"

Through the window, Susannah watched her sister stalk across the campus toward the girls' dorm. Erect, scrubbed and groomed to splendor like a prize heifer, saddle shoes polished, the strings washed weekly and rinsed in a mixture of polish and water, her hair shining from castile and lemon juice, her nails buffed and neat, her mouth maidenly pink, she was the embodiment of unyielding virtue and propriety.

Susannah sighed and went back to her sundae, closed her eyes and tried to recapture the words of her song, her hymn, her celebration of love.

"You awake?" A young man slid into the booth across from her.

"Hi, Billy Joe."

"You look all tuckered out, girl."

"I am. I'm totally exhausted. I was trying to explain to Kate about what love is, and it took up all my strength."

Billy Joe laughed and pulled one knee up onto the seat. "I know what you mean," he said sympathetically. "I tried to explain it to her once myself, and she slapped my face."

"That's the whole trouble," Susannah objected. "She thinks that's all there is to it: boys pawing at her, and having to walk home, and dirty words on the walls in the biffie." She shook her head and then asked solemnly, "Have you ever been in love, Billy Joe?"

"Sure," he answered quickly. "With Kate when I was fifteen, you when I was sixteen, Marylouise when I was seventeen, last semester with Sue Ellen and before that—"

"Silly," she interrupted. "I mean really in love—two souls with but a single thought, two hearts that beat as one, half angel and half bird, and all a wonder and a wild desire . . ."

Billy Joe leaned across the table and spoke instructively. "The female heart beats faster than the male's, Susannah. To get them to beat as one is a physical impossibility, but hey! I kinda like that wild-desire part. Where'd you get that one?"

Susannah chuckled and slumped back in the booth, smiling broadly as she considered how very good it was to know someone so well for your whole life; to have comfortable silences when you wanted them; or to let the thoughts come directly from the brain and out of the mouth without editing. She and Kate and Billy Joe had spent winters in the same rural school, summers under the same cool trees. They had shared discoveries and punishments, had gigged frogs, run trout lines, gathered blackberries for Pepper's cobblers, and had whispered about and curiously compared their differences down there. They had been children together in the lazy days of sunshine and innocence, and then one day Kate discovered sin and they did not swim naked in the pond anymore.

"Well," Susannah said, as she looked at him with the solicitude, the tenderness, of one who is about to leave another behind to embark on a long, perilous journey. "I am in love. I am half bird and half angel, and my heart beats as one with Jason Garrity's."

"Sounds mighty serious."

"It is mighty serious. I'm going to marry that man in August."

"Has he accepted your proposal?"

"Oh, he wants to marry me all right, that's obvious. But

it's in some dim, vague, way-off time when he's established and solvent and all that nonsense."

"That sounds reasonable to me."

Susannah spoke slowly for emphasis. "I'm not talking about being reasonable, Billy Joe. I'm talking about being in love."

"Being in love doesn't require any formal ceremony—"

"Yes it does," she interrupted, smiling mysteriously, "a ceremony where you commit both soul and body. . ." She frowned suddenly. "Dammit! I can't get the man into bed. Every time we get close to it, it's like he takes off his emotions and gives them a cold shower. Tell me, Billy Joe," she said urgently, reaching across the table to grip his arm. "Tell me how! How do I get him to—you know, lose control?"

Billy Joe shifted uneasily. "This is the strangest conversation I ever had with a *girl*," he said.

"You've got to help me," she insisted. "If I can't have Jason, I'll die . . . I'll die of a broken heart."

"There you go with the heart business again. You've got it all wrong. The heart doesn't break, even though the folks that put out greeting cards would have you believe it works that way."

And then Billy Joe Harris, who was held in awe and esteem from one end of the campus to the other, for his vast knowledge of the names and locations and curious functions of the body's private parts, in genuine embarrassment opened his notebook and hastily began to sketch. "You see here—" he drew a zigzag line—"they usually show it breaking from the atrium to the opposite ventricle. Sometimes a crack right down the septum." With a flourish he drew a heavy line down the center. "Very unscientific. The break—" he held up a forefinger—"pay attention, Susannah. The break occurs at the crotch of the carotid artery where it branches off from the aorta and supplies the head." He dropped his pen and leaned back with satisfaction. "You can see for yourself what happens. The oxygen supply to the brain is interfered with, causing the victim to be muddled and melancholy."

"Billy Joe. . ." she said warningly.

"As for dying of a broken heart or, more correctly, a broken carotid, as we all know the prognosis is good. Most everybody recovers by and by. Matter of fact, most people go on to repeat the accident, 'cause this is one place where good advice and experience are to no avail whatsoever."

Susannah flipped the notebook shut and slammed her hand down on top of it. "Don't sweat the mule, Billy Joe," she said firmly. "Just load the wagon." Then the stern furrows in her brow smoothed out and her voice took on a pleading tone. "Come on, help me. You're pre-med, you know all about these things. What is it that just drives a man crazy?"

Billy Joe gave a great giving-in sigh. "As a matter of fact, if I stood up right now I'd probably get arrested for indecent exposure."

Susannah looked puzzled. "You mean just talking about it?"

"Yes, ma'am. Before, during and after. And by the way, I didn't learn that in Physiology."

Susannah carefully considered this piece of information, nodded slowly, and made a mental note. "Okay," she said, all business. "I've got that, what else? And could you be a little more specific?"

"Jesus H. Christ! I don't know if I'm doin' old Jas a favor or selling him down the river." He paused and blew out his breath. "Your hands, Susannah, use your hands. Most of the time, you-all act like you got 'em tied behind you, that you're just, you know, being done to. We have to do all the preliminary work, and at great psychological risk, let me tell you! Nine chances out of ten a girl changes her mind at the crucial moment. The same girl, mind you, that's been blowin' in your ear all night on the dance floor. Here you are, pointed at the sky ready to soar, and all of a sudden it's the wrong time of the month or her daddy'll kill her or you won't respect her anymore. And if she does go all the way, she never lets you forget what a goddamn big favor she's doin' you. Believe me, Susannah, it's a real treat when somebody *participates*— you said to be specific—heaven on God's earth when you feel a little warm hand slidin' down that zipper pretty as you please and finger walkin' into your skivvies . . . Sssssss!"

Susannah was nodding energetically. "Then what?"

Billy Joe grinned wickedly. "That's it, honey. You get yourself a good hold on that—ah, that concept—and you can lead a fellow anyplace you want to take him." Susannah was still nodding, deep in thought. Billy Joe frowned and shook his head. "I feel kinda like a traitor, for some reason. Ol' Jas hasn't got a snowball's chance in hell."

Susannah looked at him archly and said in a soft voice, "What makes you think he ever did?"

"You sure this is what you want?" he went on earnestly. "Get married and have kids like ordinary folks? Susannah Warwick, the belle of Theater Arts? What happens to the big career in Hollywood?"

Susannah looked past him and through the window, past the elms that lined the walk to the library, past the bell tower, into the horizon, into the luminous future. "That was a childish thing. Now that I am a woman, I will put childish things away. I want to love Jason all the days of my life," she whispered. "To love and honor and cherish."

Billy Joe held up his hand in a mock request to speak. "There was a thing," he said pensively, "in Lit. class the other day, something about how there're two tragedies in life. One of them is not getting what you want, and the other is getting it."

But Susannah didn't hear him. Her ears were filled with her own song, her own hymn, her own celebration.

Spring came the Sunday before Easter vacation. It came suddenly and completely, dressed in tender blades of green grass and fragrant buds that were nowhere to be seen the day before. Susannah was awakened at dawn by the sound of birds in the eaves above her window. She crept close and watched them with heavy-lidded eyes as they flew in with twigs and pieces of string which they added to the odd bits of material that seemed to be the beginning of an untidy nest. They poked and thatched and fluttered, then flew off as if on a desperate errand, returning moments later to poke about again, to flutter, to utter soft sounds one to the other, to loudly scold the neighbors in the eaves at the windows down the way.

When the rays of the sun struck the windowpane and flared out in a deep orange arc, Susannah roused herself as from sleep and padded out into the hall.

"A picnic?" Jason mumbled into the telephone.

"Look out the window, dear heart! Smell the air, feel the sunshine, taste the day! Oh yes—yes!—a picnic."

"What time is it?"

"Seven. If you get your ass in gear we can be at the lake by nine. Just think, a whole unused day spread out like a bright red carpet! You there? You got stuff for sandwiches?"

"I think so," he yawned.

"Well, throw it all in a bag and let's go. I'll be in front of the dorm—the one wearing garlands and ribbons, and bowing to the east."

"Crazy woman."

"Jason?"

"Ummmmm?"

"Is that a fine idea?"

"Very fine idea. You are a crazy woman with fine ideas."

At her suggestion, Jason drove to the far side of the lake, away from the tables, the fire pits, the people. Then she shooed him away, sent him for a swim. She spread the quilt under the willows, walked up and down the shore, then made a wide circle around the spot she had chosen, to assure herself it was hidden from view. She smiled in satisfaction. It never once occurred to her that she was not in complete control, that, rather, a blueprint etched into her genes millions of years before had watched the birds that morning, had made the call, had driven to the isolated section of the lake, had searched out the deep, soft nest between the low-hanging trees, and now watched as Jason, with sure, strong strokes, his arms glistening in the sun when they cut the water, swam back from the raft at the lake's center.

She sat quietly on the sand, her chin resting on arms encircling her knees, her eyes never leaving him as he came closer and closer to shore, finally rising out of the shallow water.

He waved.

She waved back, a languid, slow greeting to this fair young Poseidon who caused tremors in her heart, this glowing god her instincts had selected to father her children.

"Stay there," she called. "I'm coming in." As he watched, in one graceful movement she stepped out of her suit, and walked slowly in her smooth nakedness, her firm resolve, toward him.

Billy Joe was right. Words did contain magic; words breathed into the ear, kissed onto the palm, bubbled out underwater in silent I-love-yous were charged with enchantment. And hands. Her fingertips moved lightly over his chest, then followed the narrow line of silky hair to the elastic band that rode low on his lean hips. He took his breath in sharply and moved away from her. "Gideon . . ." he muttered. But her hands followed him, confident, arrogant, sure of their power. "I want to feel you," she whispered. "I want to feel you inside of me, I want you to fill me up. . ."

He shuddered, then took her hand and led her, splashing, running, stumbling, to the quilt beneath the willows. Again, the spector of Gideon appeared before him, and Susannah, sensing it, constructed a flawless sentence with which to drive it away. "I will feast on thee, my love, there is no part of you my lips shall not know."

Billy Joe had spoken the truth. Jason had not a snowball's chance in hell as Susannah, "all a wonder and a wild desire," laid claim to not only his passion but his conscience as well.

It was soon after reported to Gideon in a mysterious,

unsigned note that his granddaughter had violated curfew and had been locked out of the dorm. He made the trip across the state in haste. His ongoing problems with Susannah and his conversation with the Lord regarding them were the only company he had in the waxed and polished Buick sedan. Why was it always that one? Why was there always something? Early on, she had hit on a system whereby she would look straight at her grandfather, listen intently to his instructions, and then, in open disagreement rather than disobedience proceed along a course she had previously worked out for herself. *Now* what had she done, and, more important, how had she made the kind of enemy who would stoop to anonymity, who would send an ugly printed message like the one he carried in his pocket?

He went directly to the offices and asked to have Susannah called out of class. A family matter of grave importance. Then he waited quietly, patiently: a slightly stooped, Lincolnesque figure, neat and distinguished in the well-brushed gabardine suit, vigorously shined round-toed black shoes, and closely trimmed white hair and beard.

She ran toward him. "Grampa, what is it? What's wrong?"

"I'm not quite sure, wee girl. I'd like to speak with you about it. Can we walk on the grounds?"

They walked for the better part of an hour on the sun-dappled paths that crossed and crisscrossed the campus. It had been so glorious at the lake, Susannah explained, they had simply lost track of the time. (True.) They'd had a flat tire on the way back, and the jack kept slipping. (True.) It was unavoidable, Grampa, and where was she expected to stay? She had spent the night—honest!—on Jason's couch. (True. Jason's idea. And had slept the dreamless sleep that comes of a good day's work.)

Yes, Gideon agreed, time could get away from one on such a day, and mechanical objects could be a nuisance, but it was unladylike and unforgivable for her to spend the night in Jason's rooms. Yes, indeed, Jason was a fine young man, but in the future she was to see him, or any other gentleman who might call upon her, in those places where courting was provided for. He would speak to Jason about the matter so there would be no future misunderstanding.

Jason was sternly admonished to steer clear of Babylon . . . *for those who had committed fornication and lived deliciously with her, would see the smoke of her burning.*

Suffering searing guilt and ambivalent resolve, Jason gave his word to Gideon.

Susannah reported to Billy Joe that her plans had suffered a small setback. "Only temporary," she said, smiling sweetly.

As he listened to her, he could almost hear the soft song of the sirens, behold the face that sent a thousand ships to a watery grave, see the blinded eyes of a shorn giant.

Billy Joe felt a chill reach all the way to the marrow of his breastbone, where the making of red blood cells was momentarily suspended as he rolled over in his mind one of the astounding facts of life. He swore silently right then and there that he would never—no, *never!* —fall in love. And he blessed the good fortune that had given him Susannah as a friend. A friend who told all, blurted it all out, rattled off Woman's Ancient Secrets. Did it because it didn't matter, because he was not the doomed and miserable prey she stalked.

He would certainly have to be careful—he would have to watch his step each second of all the days to come. They were *dangerous*. And devious. And bent on ownership of a man's immortal soul.

Susannah confronted her sister with the fact of the anonymous note, but was met with such genuine and convincing dismay that she all but dismissed it from a mind fully occupied with more intriguing matters.

SIX

SUSANNAH had never been, nor could she ever hope to be again, as lovely as she was the summer of her nineteenth year. She wore Jason's love with queenly radiance. It colored her cheeks, glowed in her eyes and softened her voice as she moved in a state of grace toward the appointed day.

She ordered yards of white eyelet, hand-embroidered with silver threads, and seed pearls for edging. She chose a luminous pillbox headdress with shoulder-length veil, then, as her ebullience mounted, canceled it and selected instead a pearl tiara with a cloud of netting that would fall to her feet and trail behind her as she floated down the aisle toward eternal happiness.

She agonized over silver, china and crystal patterns, and drove Pepper to distraction with demands for family recipes recorded only in Pepper's head. On ragged snatches of yellow-lined paper she scribbled love poems, freely adapted from Kahlil Gibran, Edna St. Vincent Millay and Eddy Arnold, and then, because the reality of him whom she loved could not be contained in the verses, would suddenly dash from the house to the stables and ride out, her strong brown legs gripping the bare back of the horse, in search of him.

By late June and due, for the most part, to these impromptu visits, Jason lagged behind in his summer project: replacing the fenceposts in the lower pasture. He told her not to come, and for three days she didn't, so that on the fourth day he went to her. They agreed that evening was too long in coming, so Susannah began to pack a lunch in a wicker basket and to meet him each day when the sun was overhead, at the place where the creek changed course and produced a kind of natural air-conditioning as the water splashed and sprayed off the rocks.

While he devoured half a pullet, potato salad, deviled eggs, leftover pork chops or roast beef, she would pick daintily at a chicken thigh, watching him, licking her lips when he licked his, never wondering at her lack of appetite, knowing that the real feast came after the sugar cookies and the first thermos of lemonade.

They feasted, yet Susannah's hunger was unappeased and sent her back, ravenous, the following day and the next and the next, for it was the hunger itself that delighted her, not its satisfaction. She did not tell Jason of this. She thought perhaps he would misunderstand.

She held her future before her like a sacred, shining thing. An elaborately constructed one-hundred-year plan—fluffy and pink with the substance of carnival cotton candy, conceived in euphoria, steeped in the fantasy of happy-ever-after—her design for the century made no allowances for or concessions to the unsympathetic interventions of fate, time, economics, or even her lover.

They would honeymoon in Colorado Springs: fourteen fun-filled days (just as it said on the folder); late, long, lazy breakfasts on the terrace before offering their brown young bodies to the pool, to the courts, to the mountains, to the sun, and to each other—oh yes, yes, often to each other.

They would come back to Grampa's, to the sunroom, close the door and live there and love each other while their house was being built. She would buy some marvelous Danish furniture, oiled walnut with clean straight lines, and a white couch and a king-size bed with a satin head-board. Next spring they would make a baby, a Jason-kind-of-baby, with wheat-colored hair and morning-glory eyes, a baby that would be handed over to her to nurse, to fondle, to take its toes to market, and then to hand back to a white-aproned phantom for changing.

At some later unspecified time, with their house—a white-pillared Tara sort of house, the showplace of Robina County—completed, the hands all hired, and Jason miraculously armed with an advanced degree in history, he would take a position in some fine small Eastern college. They would live in an ivy-covered, many-gabled Hawthorne kind of house where she would write haunting poetry (to be snapped up by *Harper's* and *The New Yorker),* raise bright, articulate children (to be snapped up by Harvard and Radcliffe), serve Sunday-afternoon tea to Jason's students (who would adore her), entertain with flair the young intellectuals and, with enchanting propriety the old guard. They would, of course, summer at the ranch—except for the summers spent in Rome, in the South of France, on the Greek Isles. Perhaps there wouldn't be much time for the ranch, but they could always retire there when they were old—in their fifties—and had made a hearty meal of the world.

Jason wiped the perspiration from his upper lip and flapped his hand at a fly. "Susannah, honey," he sighed, "I'll go over it one more time. Now, you pay close attention. Don't interrupt or make faces or kiss me while I'm talking. Okay?"

"I heard you the first time," she pouted.

"But it didn't register. Now, then. You listening? I have a lot of land, a small herd, and a little bit of money. I know my house isn't what you're used to, but it isn't all that bad, not as bad as you make out, and anyway we can have a lot of fun fixing it up."

"Fixing it up! Why, there isn't room in it to cuss a cat."

Jason smiled and pulled her close. "Maybe kissing is more productive, after all." He touched her forehead with his lips, and moved his hands slowly from the nape of her neck to the small of her back. "Let's go over and have a look," he murmured. "Maybe we'll get some ideas."

"What kind of ideas did you have in mind?" she answered, nuzzling his ear and pushing the length of her body hard against him. "I don't think there are any left to investigate." She pulled back and ran her forefinger over the top button of his shirt. "We may just have to start all over at the beginning—with the old missionary idea. You 'member how that one goes?"

The afternoon sun was hot. Not a blade of grass or a leaf moved in the still, humid air. The birds slept. Insects sang groggy songs of discontent. Jason drove the complaining, puffing old Chevrolet over the dirt road that separated his property from Gideon's, frowning now and then at the sound of a new rattle, a new complaint; smiling, letting out long deep breaths as Susannah's fingers softly kneaded his thigh.

Jason's father had been left the land by an uncle who had homesteaded it when Oklahoma was still a territory. Because he had no place else to go, Morgan Garrity brought his wife and young son from a meager hand-to-mouth existence in West Virginia to a meager hand-to-mouth existence in Oklahoma.

Morgan Garrity was a self-styled messenger from God who out of faith or perhaps lethargy felt he need only plant the seed, pray loudly over it, and then in good time gather in the bounty. His wife, frail and anemic, struggled with the soil in an effort to bring her husband's dreams to harvest, but the land was unyielding and unmerciful. In two winters she was dead.

Young Jason, conscientious, determined, and thirteen years old, took her place as the family provider. His days began in the lonely, dark light of 4 A.M. The chores done, he would make a breakfast of oatmeal and coarse skillet biscuits for himself and his father, then, stuffing two of the biscuits into his pocket, walk the three miles to the Warwicks', where he got a ride to school.

After school, he worked for Gideon, cleaning stalls, feeding and watering the stock, digging postholes, checking and mending fences, and learning about cattle from the best teacher the county had to offer. Then he would walk the three miles home, do his own chores, prepare supper or, more often than not, heat up what Pepper had sent with him, and later wrestle alone by kerosene light with the complexities of diagrammed sentences, algebraic proofs, and the dates of English kings.

When he was a senior in high school, two things happened—or rather, they were events of such magnitude it must be said that they transpired—to change the course of Jason's life. The first was a cloudburst. Morgan Garrity, in the habit of walking the fields as he prepared his Sunday sermons for the Greater New Canaan Church of God in Christ, was so deeply engrossed in the trials of Job, perhaps equating them with his own misfortunes, that he failed to notice the gathering clouds. Jason found his father, crushed by a fallen tree, his lifeless body shielding the Word of God.

Soon after Morgan's death, Gideon made Jason the gift of two shorthorns, a heifer and a prize seed bull, and an offer to subsidize him at Oklahoma A and M. That night Jason stayed in the barn, alternating between fitful sleep and waking wonder. For the first time, in a life that had known little other than the gray bleakness of back-breaking, unrewarding toil, he felt the sensuous rapture of tomorrow's promise.

The Garrity place had changed little in the years since Jason went off to college, off to war, back to college to complete his degree in animal husbandry, and now when he returned to put that degree into practice.

The front porch faced the road, but had a bare and unused look to it. Grass grew in the dooryard in the spring and died quickly in the summer heat. A red-dust path led from the car barn, past the well and the smokehouse, to the kitchen door. The kitchen ran the length of the house, with one door leading to an aboveground cellar, the other to a parlor and a curtained-off bedroom. Jason had painted the inside walls the summer before, but age and weather had claimed the outside for their own.

In the parlor, three daybeds served as couches, and four old rockers surrounded the fat woodburning stove. An elderly Montgomery Ward linoleum covered part of the graying wood floor, and curtains, sewn up clumsily by Jason himself out of faded checked flour sacks, hung limp and cheerless at the windows.

Susannah stood in the middle of the parlor and surveyed her castle. Her shoulders fell as she thought of oiled Danish and Hawthorne gables.

"Oh, it's awww-ful," she cried. "Just God-awful!"

"We can get some new furniture," Jason said, with the tone one uses to placate a disappointed child. "New coat of paint, new curtains—why, you won't even know it's the same place."

"It smells," Susannah said flatly.

Jason sniffed the air and shook his head. "I don't smell anything."

"It smells old—and musty."

"It may be only a year, honey. I'd figured on two, but maybe I can swing it in one."

"But why do we have to wait? Grampa would loan us the money. He'd probably give it to us."

Jason drew himself up, looking slightly pained. "Now, isn't that just dandy. I ask him for his granddaughter, then I turn around and ask him to put a roof over her head."

Susannah frowned, then her face brightened, as if it had just come clear to her how really simple the solution was.

"A lot of people help their kids get started."

"I'm not a kid, Susannah." He met and held her eyes. He would go just so far with the placating game, and they both knew it.

She turned away from him. "Oh, Jason! Dammit! I don't want to fight with you. But things aren't turning out the way we talked about them. Remember what you said about getting a degree in history and teaching?"

Jason smiled. "And do you remember when we had that conversation?"

"Vividly. It was that Sunday at the lake."

"It was wishful thinking, Susannah, wishful talk from a man who's seen a little bit of the world and puzzles about it and wonders how it got that way. Sometimes a man dreams out loud about all the things he'd like to do, but life just isn't long enough. You have to make a choice, have to decide which dream you can make come true."

"But you have a good, strong minor in history. It wouldn't take long—"

"Too long. I'll be twenty-six in September. I've got to get on with it."

"Oh, Jason! I thought it was all settled."

"You mean you had settled it in your head." He took her hands and led her to one of the daybeds. His expression was urgent, electric. "Look, honey, I'm not going to be a dirt farmer with a few head of shorthorns. I'm going to be a *breeder*, going to get myself a Santa Gertrudis and breed him to a Highlander. I'm going to create the finest breed of beef cattle in this world. Why, we'll have the biggest herd in the country outside of Kingsville. You take a weight gainer like a Santa Gertrudis, cross him with a forager like a Highlander—"

He paused as he saw her eyes wander past him, fixed on other dreams.

"Is it money?" he questioned. "My God, as far as that goes, in a few years you'll be able to light your cigarettes with five-dollar bills if you're a mind to. Travel? Just pick up the phone and say, 'I'm Mrs. Jason Garrity, the beautiful wife of the cattle mogul, and I'd like two first-class tickets on your next flight to Madagasdar. No space? Unacceptable! To whom, my good man, do I speak regarding the purchase of the airlines?'"

He rushed on, encouraged by the small smile that played across her face. "Don't you see, honey? This is me—land and stock. This is my work."

Susannah sighed deeply and took a cigarette from Jason's shirt pocket. He lit a match with his thumbnail, held it for her, then eased her down on the bed, his hand resting lightly on her breast, his mouth in the hollow of her throat.

"You must be crazy with the heat, Jason Garrity."

"Now what?"

She took a long, dramatic drag from the cigarette, and blew the smoke directly in Jason's face.

"All things considered," she said slowly, "I figure I already had one good screwin' today."

She hauled herself off the bed, marched out of the house and to the car, where she waited, haughty and imperious, as if for a footman to open the door.

Jason swore to himself as he followed her out.

July boiled and bubbled over into August. Heavy wet heat took its toll of energies and tempers. In the sunroom, a dress form wore Susannah's wedding gown, and every morning Gran removed the tissue-paper swathing to add more tiny seed pearls.

Susannah was engulfed in preparations. She made lists, crossed off completed chores with almost military precision, filed them away and made new lists. Not a stone was left unturned, a task undone, with the notable and glaring exception of Jason's house. When he would speak of it (What color would she like the parlor? When was she going to get new curtains? Would she like him to take the daybeds out and get a divan and chair? How 'bout painting the rockers bright red or something?) she would blink and visibly close her mind to his words.

Silently, she told herself to be sensible, to be realistic, that the house, after all, wasn't all that important, that there was plenty of time for stained glass and oiled walnut.

"I'll go over there tomorrow," she would tell herself, "and measure those windows." Then tomorrow would dawn, and the distaste for the old house, the rancor at being offered no choice, would well up unbidden and swallow her fine resolutions.

The second week in August, just two weeks before the wedding date, Gran took a hand in the matter. They were in the sunroom stitching on the last of the pearls.

"Well," said Gran, looping the white thread around her forefinger and bending over to break it neatly with her teeth. "Now this is done you'll be able to tend to Jason's house."

"Ummm."

"I have near a bolt of Indianhead that'll make up fine for curtains in the parlor."

"Um hum."

"You ought to see to that tomorrow. Time's aflying." She peered at her granddaughter's fair head bent over her work in exaggerated concentration. "Don't you reckon?"

"It'd be a waste of good cotton to put curtains in that dump."

The old woman leaned back in her chair. "It's Jason's home. It's what he has to offer you for the time being."

"He has money."

"He needs it to enrich his stock."

"But we could at least start on the house, at least make some plans about it."

"To Jason's way of thinking, that's not the way to do it."

"That doesn't mean he's right!" Susannah jabbed her needle into the pincushion and folded her arms across her chest.

"If you don't think the man's right," Gran said evenly, "if you can't believe in him and be some help and comfort to him, then chances are you won't make him much of a wife."

The arms folded themselves tighter. "Gran, why did you and Grampa bother to send me to school if you're so dead set against my thinking for myself, having some opinions about things?"

"Thinking for yourself is fine, Missy, all except where a husband's concerned. Then if you have thoughts for yourself that's contrary to his, you do well to keep them to yourself."

Susannah wiped little beads of perspiration from her forehead. It was early and cool. "That's absolutely medieval. Don't you know what year this is, Gran? Women have equality now."

Gran smiled, and her pale-blue eyes twinkled behind her

silver-rimmed glasses. "Pity too," she said. "In the old days they had superiority, and it's a poor exchange, to my way of thinking. As for sending you to college, it's good for a woman to have an education. She can help her children with their lessons, and she can teach if times get hard or the Lord takes her husband from her."

"But nothing for herself?"

"What is it you want for yourself, Susannah?"

"I'm not sure. . ."

"Do you love Jason? Do you want to marry him and raise a family?"

"Oh yes, Gran—yes! But that doesn't mean I want the world to stop turning. I don't want to have a whole slew of barefoot kids and live out here in the middle of nowhere for the rest of my life. I really didn't know how serious Jason was about the ranch. He'd get so, I don't know, *transported* when he talked about studying history and teaching it. He made it sound so exciting—teaching young minds about the past so the future of the world could be better. It was like a dream, and I felt that I was going to share in it. Share in a fine adventure, in a great quest!" She frowned and pouted in turns, then added ruefully, "I just can't get the same feeling over the prospect of raising cattle and shipping them off to the stockyards."

Gran looked at Susannah closely. "Maybe," she said pointedly, "maybe you need a dream of your own."

"Oh no, Gran! I do love him. I want to share his life, but I want it to be full and exciting. When we were there a couple of weeks ago and Jason was going on about painting and curtains and all that, all I could think of was how it smelled—old, old and dead. And I got this vision of myself, an old woman with my hair pulled back and a funny old catalogue dress, never been anyplace or seen anything or done anything, just another farmer's wife."

"Is that the way you see me?"

Susannah jumped up from her chair and knelt in front of her grandmother, taking the rough, wrinkled hands in the smooth young ones. "No, Gran—no, no. This is the life you wanted, but there are so many more worlds to choose from now."

"But if Jason was to agree to start on the house, then that would make a difference?"

"Yes! Don't you see? It would mean that we could at least compromise."

Gran was quiet, deep in thought. It was partly her own doing, she realized that—hers and Gideon's. But this had been such an easy child to love and to indulge, to give in to. It was their fault that Susannah thought the act of compromise meant simply having her own second choice in a matter.

"Well," Gran said, "if a new house is what you want, I can tell you, you're going way around the barn to get it. My stars, girl, you're going at Jason head on. You gotta ease up on his good side. Now, if he saw that you were willing to give in now and then, instead of all the time being ornery and headstrong and demanding your rights, then he'd take more kindly to your ideas about a house, or anything else, for that matter. You put the man in a corner and you give him no room to back down in—not honorably. I don't give a hang what the Congress said. The Lord said, 'He shall rule over thee,' and I think you just better start from there."

She put her hands on her knees and rose slowly to her feet. "Let's just have a look at that Indianhead, Missy."

Susannah measured the windows. She bought a Sears, Roebuck rug and shopped for a divan and an easy chair. To her surprise, she felt a twinge of satisfaction in watching a new room emerge from the old.

She was hanging the crisp new curtains when a truck drove up to the front gate.

"Jason Garrity's place?" a man yelled from the cab.

"He's in the field," Susannah yelled back. "Won't be home till late this afternoon."

"You Miz Garrity?"

"Damn near," Susannah laughed. "Next week."

The man got out of the truck and walked up the path.

Susannah stepped out on the front porch to meet him. He thrust some papers toward her.

"Can you sign for this?" he asked. "And look 'im over, make sure he's in one piece?"

"Sign for what?"

"Mighty fancy bull, all the way from Kingsville."

Susannah craned her neck and looked past the man to the truck.

"I didn't know Jason bought another. . ." Her voice trailed off. "You sure you got the right place? You sure it's for Garrity?"

"This his signature?"

She looked at the familiar hand and saw above it the amount typed in the balance column. The bill of sale was stamped paid.

"Yes," she said angrily. "I'll sign for him, and I'll look him over. I've never seen a bull that cost that kind of money. What's he got? Gold teeth?"

The man winked. "Reckon the gold is located nearer the other end," he said, laughing.

She didn't take time to saddle the horse, nor did she stop to hook the barbed-wire gate behind her. A tunnel of gray dust followed her through the upper pasture, then along the creek and to the irrigated green bottom land where Jason rested under a great oak, munching an apple and entertaining visions of an empire. He started up at the sight of the lathered horse.

"What's the matter? What is it?" he called, running to meet her.

"Where did you get the money?" she screamed at him. "You told me there was no more money."

"Will you please get down from there and tell me what you're yelling about?"

She refused his hand, swung her leg around and slid off frontward. "I'm talking about fifteen thousand dollars on the hoof! I saw the bill of sale, Jason. It was marked *paid!*"

"That's no reason to kill a good horse. You know better

than to ride like that in this heat. Gideon'd have your hide—"

"We're not talking about my hide or my grandfather. We're talking about you—you! You cheated me, Jason, you cheated me and you lied to me. You told me there wasn't enough money to start on a house. You gave me a budget that wouldn't furnish a chicken coop, and you wouldn't let me spend my own money. You sliced a week off Colorado Springs because it costs too much, and then you turn around and buy that goddamn bull!"

Jason spoke quietly and evenly. "I have not lied to you, Susannah, or cheated you. I've been negotiating for that bull for over two months—you knew about it. It's just that you have not listened to one word from me that you didn't want to hear." He put his hands on her shoulders and leaned close. "Listen! That's no ordinary bull; that's the natural descendant of the first Santa Gertrudis bred on the King Ranch. He's an investment in our future—"

"Oh shut up!" she bawled at him, wiggling out of his grasp. Then she twisted the small diamond off her finger and flung it at his feet. "Put that through the bull's nose—I hope the two of you will be very happy."

She rode back more slowly, mindful of the horse, shivering in righteous fury. She hooked the gate, turned the horse into the barnyard, spat in the direction of the stall that housed the natural descendant of the King Ranch's first Santa Gertrudis, then climbed into Gideon's Buick and started home.

Kate met her at the door and stopped her angry words with white-faced shock. "He's gone," she said in a hollow voice. "Grampa's gone."

"Gone?"

"He's—he's—passed away. It just happened. Just now."

They stared at each other, not believing it. It was not possible, both of them knew that. There was some mistake. They had never seen him with anything more serious than a head cold, and he had the strength and energy of a man half his age. Gideon was immortal. Everyone knew that.

"He just . . . slipped away," Kate said finally. "He asked me to get the afghan for his feet, said they were cold. When I got back with it, I thought he was sleeping—his eyes were closed and he looked so peaceful. I started to spread the afghan over him, then I realized. . ."

Tears stood in her eyes and she lifted her shoulders in a gesture of profound helplessness. "Oh dear God!" she cried. "He's gone—Grampa's gone. . ."

Their need to share the loss, and to deny it, brought Jason and Susannah close. On the night of Gideon's death, they made love in the heat of that need. The quarrel, the spite and bitterness, the ongoing battle for the upper hand—these were put aside, displaced by an awesome struggle to reaffirm life.

The white dress was gently and lovingly folded, wrapped in a tissue-paper shroud and laid to rest in an old trunk in the attic. "My daughter will wear it," Susannah said sadly. Decisions were made easily and without issue. The fun-filled days in Colorado were canceled by mutual consent. Instead, they would drive to Arkansas and be married there by a justice the weekend after the reading of Gideon's will. That was long enough to wait—proper enough—and a weekend was better than nothing.

Susannah told Jason that at least now there would be no need for them to stew and fret over money matters, for surely there would be a great deal of money. And since, at least for the time being, he would have to run not only his own place but the Warwick Ranch as well, of course it would be sensible to live in the big house . . . of course.

"We'll see," Jason had answered, and the matter was closed.

But it was far from closed in Susannah's mind. She was unable to reconcile the loss of her grandfather with the gains that had come as a result of it. In the hot, dark night she would awaken with voices whispering to her that the problem was solved now, that she had won. And she would cover her ears, bury her face in the pillow and scream soundlessly that she had loved him, that she had not wished him dead.

SEVEN

I N THE name of God, I, Gideon Thomas Warwick of Robina County in the sovereign state of Oklahoma, being of sound mind and better shape physically than I have a right to expect at my age, but also paying heed to the uncertainty of life and the certainty of death, and remembering it is appointed for all men to die, do make and ordain this to be my last Will and Testament in the manner and form following.

Suffice it to say that I act solely on the dictates of my own heart and conscience.

First I give my soul into the hands of Almighty God who gave it, and my body to the earth to be buried in a decent manner after the direction of my executor here-inafter named, and as for my worldly estate which it has pleased the Lord to bestow upon me, I give and bequeath it in the following manner:

Item: I give and bequeath to my beloved wife, Eve-lina Page Warwick, all my monies, all my lands, the dwellings thereon with their furnishings and appoint-ments, and the livestock and crops with the exceptions noted hereinafter, for her to have the use, profits and income thereof so long as she shall live. Upon her death these same lands, dwellings, furnishings, appointments, livestock and crops, with the exceptions noted hereinafter, are to pass to my granddaughter Catherine Margaret Warwick, her heirs and assigns forever.

Item: I give and bequeath to my granddaughter Susannah Sarah Warwick the sum of fifty thousand dollars to be held in trust by my wife, Evelina, and issued in whatever manner she deems fit and proper until said granddaughter has attained her twenty-fifth year. Should my wife meet her death before Susannah's twenty-fifth birthday, it is my wish that Susannah receive the full amount due her at that time, with the suggestion that she use it wisely and with more care than is her wont to do. Also, I give and bequeath to my granddaughter Susannah the oil rights on all my properties, including the local three sections and the property north of the Verduga River in Newton County which I purchased on speculation in 1940 and sold to Ed Bridges in 1944, retaining all mineral rights as is duly recorded at the county seat. Both rights and income from said rights are to be held in trust by my wife in the manner outlined above. Also, I give and bequeath to Susannah my Appaloosa mare, Bright Feather. This is a needless bequest on my part, as Susannah is the only one who can stay up on the contrary beast anyways. So be it.

Item: I give and bequeath to my friend and employee, Pepper Hawley, the sum of ten thousand dollars. Also, I give and bequeath to Pepper the original Warwick house, the frame dwelling she has occupied since the Lord in His graciousness sent her to join this family, and also the adjoining five-acre field for her to have the use, profits and income thereof so long as she shall live. Upon her death the house and five acres are to revert to my granddaughter Catherine, her heirs and assigns forever.

Item: I give and bequeath anything I might have left

put or forgotten or overlooked to my wife, Evelina, as she has been picking up after me all these years, for which I give thanks to God, to Evelina, and to my good fortune.

Item: My will is that my wife pay my just and lawful debts.

Lastly I do nominate, constitute and appoint Evelina, Executor of this my last Will, revoking all other Wills, bequests and legacies made by me and confirm this to be my last Will and Testament.

Nat Apperson, lawyer and lifetime family friend, was well aware of the mounting tension as he read from the handwritten will. He had, in fact, when he witnessed it, argued with Gideon about the document's unfairness to Susannah, but Gideon had held firmly to the conviction that to split the property would surely result in Susannah's half being sold off before he and Gran were cold in their graves. Now, as Apperson intoned the last words of Gideon's legacy, he glanced nervously at the younger granddaughter in anticipation of the storm to follow.

She met his glances—leaning forward, elbow on crossed knee, chin in hand—with birdlike fixity.

"And that's that," Apperson said, clearing his throat. "I think Gideon, as usual, has made everything pretty clear, but if you have any questions—"

"I have a question," Susannah interrupted. "Why have I been turned out of the house I was born in?"

"Now, Susannah, you know very well that was not your grandfather's intent. He meant it to be your home for as long as you wish it."

"That's not what he wrote down on that paper."

"Well, after all, he made this will after you and Jason announced your engagement. You had no need of the house. Actually, he's been very generous, what with the cash and the oil rights—"

"To be doled out by Gran if I'm a good girl. I'm not buying that, Mr. Apperson. He must have had a reason for doing it this way. What was it?"

Apperson removed his spectacles and polished them with a large white handkerchief. "Susannah," he said slowly, "your grandfather believed that you had no real interest, no deep feeling for the land and what he had made of it. There's no question of his abiding affection for you, but he wanted to keep the land whole for his great-grandsons and their sons to follow. He was afraid that you didn't understand that."

Susannah stood up quickly, her bag and gloves dropping from her lap, and pointed an accusing finger at Kate. "Leave it to Saint Catherine over there and there won't even *be* any great-grandsons!"

"All right, Susannah," Gran said warningly, "there's no call for that kind of talk. It was your grampa's to give, however he saw fit. Thank you, Nat. I'd take it kindly if you'd stop by the house one day next week so we can do what Gideon wanted. I'm tired now and I'd like to go home."

Susannah spent the afternoon behind the locked door of the sunroom. She ignored the dinner bell and had to be both cajoled and mildly threatened when Pepper later brought up a tray.

"Open up this door, Susannah! Land sakes, you actin' like some kinda snotnose kid." There was no response. Pepper sighed and sweetened her voice. "Open up now, Missy. I made some nice milk toast and a custard with brown-sugar syrup."

The silence continued, then there was a rustle and the sound of the key in the lock. Susannah blocked the doorway as she held out her arms for the tray.

"I think I'll come in an' set a spell," Pepper said, moving quickly into the room.

"I don't want to talk to anybody."

"Who said anything about talkin'? I jest wanta rest my achin' feet." She carried the tray to the sewing machine and set it down. "Here, now, wee girl, have this toast 'fore it gits cold."

The endearment—her grandfather's for her—was too

much for Susannah. She sank into the rocker, hugged her shoulders and sobbed. "It's like being left out," she moaned brokenly. "All this time I thought he loved me best, but he didn't love me at all. He didn't give a hoot about the money and that's what he left me, something he didn't even care about. It was this place he loved, the house and the land, and he's given it all to Kate, right down to the last chicken!" She looked up at Pepper, her eyes wide, her lower lip trembling. "He gave everything that meant anything to him to Kate."

Pepper crossed quickly to the rocker and pressed Susannah's head against her stomach. "Now, you're wrong there, Missy. Gideon had a healthy respect for money, and it gave him a whole lot of pleasure. An' he gave you Bright Feather, an' you know how he loved that crazy horse. Why, your granddaddy's will shows jest how much he did care for you. Can't you see that? You sharin' this land with Kate woulda been like puttin' a bit in your mouth an' sure as anythin' you'd a chomped at it till you got shed of it. Now, that don't mean you cain't stay here if you a mind to. You free to do jest as you please, and God knows ain't many folks gits that chance."

Susannah burrowed deeper into Pepper's apron, accepting the patting, the smoothing, the clucking. Then she sniffed the air and looked with some interest toward the tray on the Singer.

"I guess maybe I am hungry, just a little." She ate the milk toast in silence and, halfway through the brown-sugar custard, slowed up to ask, "Where's Jason?"

"He and Kate went over to his place. The new bull's got the miseries."

"What's wrong?"

"Don' know."

"Why'd Kate have to go?"

"Why not?"

Susannah frowned. "She's just been aching for a chance to be some sort of help to him."

Pepper threw her head back and laughed loudly. "Now, ain't nobody could 'cuse *you* a that." She picked up the tray and held it in front of Susannah. "Take your tea there. I'll tell Jason to come on up when he gits back."

It was a quarter of nine when she heard the unmistakable rattles and snorts of the old Chevy. She had spent the evening in the gathering darkness of her own thoughts, weighing the facts and sorting the feelings. Pepper was right. She was no help to him. Gran's words were equally true. At this rate, she wasn't going to make him much of a wife. She had thought only of what she wanted. But now she would try, she really would try!

She heard voices in the lower hall, then heavy footsteps on the stairs. When she opened the door for him, Jason's face was dull and without greeting. His hair was wet, his clothes looked as if he'd come through a summer shower, he smelled of sweat and damp hay.

"Come sit down, hon," she said, pulling him gently into the room. "Pepper getting you something to eat?"

He shook his head wearily. "I'm on my way to pick up some stuff for the vet. I thought you might want to go."

"What's wrong?"

"We don't know yet. The vet thinks there may be a perforation. We just don't know." He fell into the rocker and beat at the palm of his hand with his fist. "If I lose this bull—oh God, if I lose this bull. . ."

"Maybe he was sick when they sent him. Maybe they're the one's responsible." Jason's head was still shaking slowly from side to side. "What else did the vet say? Jason?"

"I told you! He says he doesn't know."

"You don't have to yell at me. I was just trying—"

"It's nothing personal, Susannah. I'm tired and I just don't know what to do. Goddammit! You bust your ass and . . ."

Susannah shrugged her shoulders and smiled brightly. "I don't see what there is to worry about. He's insured, isn't he? And even if he wasn't, I'm sure Gran would turn loose of the pursestrings for anything as important as a seed bull."

Jason blanched and he rubbed the side of his head as if he

didn't believe his own ears. "Would you please stop that," he said. His words were low and quiet, but Susannah could hear the deep roar beneath them. "Do not," he went on, pouncing on each word, using his finger for emphasis, "do *not* throw your fucking money in my face one more time. I've had all I can stomach of the big heiress routine."

Susannah backed away from him, looking resentful and tragic. She opened her mouth to speak, but Jason had not finished.

"That animal—that *particular* animal—is special. I researched the line, I studied the breeding records all the way back to God. He's the best. I don't want the insurance money, I don't want another bull, I want this one to live. Goddammit! Kate understands this, why can't you?"

There was an awkward pause as Susannah felt more and more discomfort, more unsure of herself. "I was trying to be helpful," she said finally, very quietly. "It just didn't come out that way."

Jason sighed, closed his eyes and leaned back. "We won't be able to go this weekend," he muttered. "We can wait till next week or we can be married at the courthouse in Martinsville. Whichever you want is okay with me."

She struggled with her rising anger, but Jason's words, coming as they did on the heels of her self-chastisement and fresh-scrubbed resolutions, were a call to arms, an inflammatory summons to a point of no return.

She began to pace up and down the room.

"Now, then," she said, with an air of bringing order to the discussion. "Let me run over this again, let me make sure that I understand you." She held up a forefinger and pushed it back with the fingers of her other hand. "The original plan, you may recall, was for two weeks in Colorado Springs. Correct? But then you bought this, this *sickly* bull, so there was money only for one week. Right?"

She stepped directly in front of him and leaned down so her nose almost touched his. "Then Grampa died." She pulled back, eyes flashing, and thrust a wagging finger in his face. "He died, Jason, all on his own, so you needn't try to make me feel guilty about it. Of course we couldn't go. I wouldn't have left Gran, but it suited you fine anyway. Well, what else? Let's see. We couldn't spend any money on that old shack because of—the bull. Now we can't go to Shadowlake because of—the bull. You've got your back up at me right now because of—the bull! What do you figure will be next on the list because of that fifteen-thousand-dollar disaster?"

He came out of the chair, shaking. "What does it matter?" he yelled at her. "What the hell does it matter if we make it legal this week or next? If we do it here or fifty miles away?" A thin, cold smile played across his face as he went on. "Or did you plan to make a three-act play out of it with you as the born-again virgin—soft music and a pink nightie and an hour in the can to prepare for the big deflowering?" He looked away in disgust and repeated, "What the hell does it matter?"

She took a step backward, knocked off balance by the sting of his words. "But, Jason," she said, her eyes filling, "it's our wedding, the beginning of our life together. It does matter."

He felt the prickly nudges of regret as he watched the tears stand in her eyes and start to slip down her cheeks. She looked so frail and helpless and—what else? What was it, that look? *Needy.* That was the word! Her eyes were two gray wounds in her face; he squeezed his own shut when visions of old beaten dogs came to him. About as helpless as a bitch fox, he reminded himself; as needy as a badger. Suddenly the truth came on him like a great white light. Gideon was right to leave the land to the one who would appreciate it, the one who collected the 4-H ribbons, who showed the prize Plymouth Rocks, the one who could whisper kindness into the ear of a mighty bull, her eyes shining with the glow of purity. The one who tended the garden, not the one who brought apples at noon.

He kept his eyes closed as he spoke, to keep her out, to keep the beaten dog at bay, to see on the underside of his lids the fox and the badger. "Really?" he said. "It really matters where and when we say a few words? Belated words?"

She swallowed hard and brushed at her tears. "Do you," she stammered, "do you hold it against me because I've let you make love to me?"

"Let?" he said harshly. "Can you really bring yourself to use the word *let*? Well, by damn, the lady can blush! Listen! I promised Gideon man to man on my honor, gave him my word, but there you were all over me like some alley cat coming on heat. I haven't even got that fence done for servicing you all summer long—"

Her scream split the night. "That's enough, Jason," she whispered. "No more—please—no more."

She packed only what would fit into the three bags; bags fragrant and bright with newness. The dainty lingerie from the happy-ever-after dream was folded and placed in a bottom drawer. The gown and the peignoir, fluid and flowing and, yes, pink, were touched, kneaded lightly between fingers and thumb and then hung in the closet beside the blue silk going-away suit.

She set her bags at the top of the stairs, then knocked on her grandmother's bedroom door. "You awake, Gran?"

The voice came back. "What time is it?"

"It's late, Gran. I have to talk to you."

"Come in, come in."

Susannah opened the door and stood for a moment in the doorway, a dark silhouette in the dim light from the hall.

Gran pulled herself up, turned on the light, plumped the pillows behind her, then took her glasses from the table beside the bed and hooked them over her ears. Her hair was down, gray-white close to the scalp, yellowing where it spilled over her lawn cotton shoulders.

"I reckon," she said, "from the sound of it, that wasn't an ordinary lover's spat."

"I'm leaving."

Gran looked her up and down: the white pumps, the navy dress usually worn for shopping in the city. "And where did you plan to leave to at this time of night?"

"I want your permission to take the car to the station. Kate can pick it up tomorrow. I'll take the morning train to

Kansas City, and I can get the Santa Fe there for Los Angeles." She paused and took a deep breath. "I'm asking you to give me some of my money."

"Wait till morning," Gran said wearily. "Folks say things in the night, things they don't really mean. It'll all look different in the light of day. We'll talk about it then."

Susannah was shaking her head back and forth while her grandmother spoke, and, when she finished, said quietly, "No. No, I will not be humiliated, and I will not spend another night in this house as a guest."

"You know that's not true. None of it."

"I don't know that. I don't know that at all."

Gran sighed. "You're set on going?"

"Yes, ma'am."

"And where will you stay? What will you do?"

"Marylouise has a cousin out there. She said we were welcome to visit anytime. I'll get a job. I'm going to have a career. I'm going to be important."

Gran knew the look, the stance, knew them well. The lifted chin, the soft bulge at the back of the jaw from teeth clenched down on unspeakable rage, the level gaze, the fists at the end of stiff arms held close to the sides, the knuckles whitening. She had watched the same look settle over Gideon from time to time, had seen it in Adam when he told his father with deadly calm that he would, even if Gideon *did* disown him, he would marry Elizabeth Sullivan.

There was no question about it, Susannah was leaving.

"And if I don't give you the money?" Gran asked, grasping at a straw she knew did not exist.

"Then I'll get it from Pepper. If she won't give it to me, I'll borrow it from Mr. Apperson and sign a note to pay him back when you die."

Gran smiled indulgently, shaking her head slowly from side to side. Her eyes, red-rimmed, blinked behind her glistening spectacles. She patted the side of the bed, then held out her arms as she spoke. "Come here, come here to me. You're like a wild animal that's been wounded and strikes out at everything around it. Come here, Missy. I'll give you the money, but I'm too old to be threatened with the prospect of my own passing."

Susannah laid her face next to her grandmother's and sobbed into the pillow. "Oh Gran, it hurts so . . . it *hurts*."

Gran's arms formed a protective circle around her; strong lean arms, muscular for a woman, a woman of her years, covered with reddish freckles and larger liver-colored blotches, and small scars that had healed in raised white designs; arms that would have been both shield and sanctuary for as long as there was strength in them. If they could have. Which she knew they could not. Knew also that this pain in this child, this first real anguish, would provide its own measure of immunity and after this would never again slice with such cruel accuracy to the center of the heart.

She ran her hand over Susannah's tangled hair, over her heaving shoulders, and she hummed tunelessly as one does to a fretful child who is almost but not quite asleep.

EIGHT

SUSANNAH SET the gold-framed picture back on the dressing table and with dazed effort returned herself to the haunted yellow room.

"It's over and done with," she told the three smiling faces. "We all got what we wanted."

She slipped down the stairs, through the dining room and into the kitchen. Pepper's broad back was to her, tensed in the absorption of coaxing Jell-O out of a mold onto a bed of curly endive. How she had wanted Pepper with her! How she had begged, pleaded and threatened. First it was Gran who could not be left, then the babies, one by one, and finally, two years ago, it was simply that her bones were too old to be chasing around the country-side. Besides, in case a body needed her, it was better if they knew where to look. Independent little baggage like Susannah didn't need no lookin' after anyways.

"You are most surely a Watusi," Susannah had told her once, with young and patronizing certainty, and then had regaled her with a lavish mixture of fact and fiction about a tribe of handsome giants who had emigrated from Egypt to

Africa and were perhaps descended from King Solomon himself.

"I'm American, same as you," was Pepper's answer, and she directed Susannah to hush up her nonsense and do her geometry before it got cold.

Twenty years later, Susannah still harbored the notion that Pepper's ancestors had worn the purple. Just under six feet tall, with one hundred and seventy-five pounds distributed smoothly over a slender, long-limbed frame, Pepper—as Susannah had good reason to know—could not be outrun, outtalked, or outsmarted.

The Jell-O made a sucking sound and plopped onto the plate. Pepper let out the breath she'd been holding to insure a neat unmolding and began to sing softly.

> "Jesus walked this lonesome valley,
> He had to walk it by hisself.
> Nobody else could walk it for him,
> He had to waaaaaaalk—"

And then she saw her. "Missy! Oh, my darlin' baby! I thought you was nappin'." She wiped her hands on her apron, and they fell into each other's arms. "Poor baby," she crooned, "my poor baby without no momma." These were the same words she had always used for a variety of hurts and failings. Almost any condition from a skinned knee to a picky appetite could be tied in with Elizabeth's absence from the household.

"Poor Momma, Pepper. What about poor Momma?"

"She with the Lord now. Our Savior heals the sick ones, and poor Lizbeth's been sick in her soul since your daddy passed over. She with your daddy now and our sweet Lord Jesus. Don't you fret, her troubles is over." She hugged Susannah closer, then held her at arm's length. "Let me look atcha! Mercy! Skinny as a winter rabbit, and dark circles round your eyes."

Susannah stepped back, spread her arms wide and looked down at herself. "This," she said dramatically, "is what is known as svelte. And this," she blinked her eyes rapidly, "is my fashionable eye makeup."

Pepper narrowed her own eyes and pretended to take a better look. "Do tell? Well, you looks to me a little like the orphan pictures in the magazines. But I reckon we can fatten you up, an' we got soap and water to spare."

Susannah grinned broadly. "The years go by and you still treat me like I haven't got good sense."

Pepper chuckled. "That's 'cause you ain't." Then she opened a drawer in the cabinet and took out an apron. "Here," she said, flapping the creases out of it and handing it to Susannah, "you get to cleanin' them radishes. Maybe a hundred folks here today an' I's behind in my business."

Susannah tied the apron strings behind her, ran water over the radishes, then took a paring knife from the rack over the sink. "Is Kate okay? She seems awfully pale."

"Kate's fine," Pepper answered quickly. "She's just all tired out from feelin' guilty. Takes on 'bout what she coulda done and shoulda done and woulda done if things had been different. I tell her if a frog had wings he wouldn't be so apt to bump his bottom when he jumps. But her heart's sore and they ain't no reachin' her."

She peered over her glasses at the radish flowers Susannah had started to carve. "You better just cut 'em in half, Missy, or they won't be enough to go round. Grief and sorrow seems to get a body ever' place but in the stomach. Land, you shoulda seen 'em eat yesdiddy! Some of the ladies bring stuff, so it ain't so bad." She sniffed disdainfully. "Ladies that ain't spoke a kind word to your poor momma for twenty-five years is all over the place with casseroles and Christian forgiveness. They's cucumbers in the Frigidaire when you finishes that. Anyways, you know your sister, once she gets a good hold on a notion, there's no jarrin' her loose, and she's got it in her head that if she'd been a better daughter, more charitable 'bout your momma's failin's, then the Lord wouldn't a taken her away. Don't take the peelin' off, that's where all the good vitamins is."

"What does she think she could have done?"

"For one thing, she thinks she shoulda let her have the whiskey out in the open 'stead a Jason sneakin' it to her."

"Jason?"

"Jason and Hodge cooked it up betweenst them. Two of the softest, sweetest hearts the Lord ever made." Pepper raised her long forefinger and spoke sternly. "'Course it was wrong, but they meant it as a kindness." Her finger came down and pointed to the refrigerator. "They's a nice potato salad there, and you can dish up some of them spiced peaches in the pantry."

Susannah started across the room to the twin refrigerators. Pepper turned, leaned against the cabinet and folded her arms across her breast. Her face creased into a deep thoughtful frown. "I think it goes back a lot further—what she's feelin' so shameful about, I mean. Lizbeth would come when they was a new baby, and she'd stay four-five months ever' time. She waited on Kate hand and foot and got up of a night with the babies. And that Patrick! He had the colic—mercy!

"She never touched a drop, neither. Your momma never touched a drop whilst she was lookin' after them babies. But you never heard words so mean and ugly as the things Kate said to her."

Susannah stood still in the middle of the floor, holding the bowl of potato salad. "What was it? What was wrong?"

Pepper licked her lips and turned back to the counter. She picked up a damp dishcloth and began vigorously to wipe the surface.

"Pepper?"

"Oh, I don' know, Missy. Dr. Bill said it had somethin' to do with hormones."

"But what do *you* think?"

"Well, for one thing, callin' him Dr. Bill 'stead of Billy Joe don't give me any more confidence in what he knows 'bout female complaints. Why, the man ain't even got a wife!"

"That counter is slick as a whistle, Pepper. Come on. What do you think?"

Pepper looked at the counter, smiled sheepishly, and turned to face Susannah. "Well, it 'pears to me that them hormones an' all is jest Mother Nature goin' about her business. I think what was wrong had been wrong for a long time. I reckon that Kate in her whole life never had somebody that she figured loved her the best. When she was a youngun, it must of seemed to her there weren't enough to go round after you got your share. That ain't true, but it's been like a deep affliction.

"Then here'd come along these little creatures dependin' on her, dependin' on her to open up her heart to 'em, and she jest didn't know how, didn't even know where to start.

"So, her momma done it. I'd see Kate watchin' her sometimes. Lizbeth's rockin' 'em, singin' 'em to sleep, lovin' 'em, and I could almost see Kate thinkin', behind her eyes, way back in a secret place she'd given over to them kinds of black thoughts, *Where was you . . .?*"

"But Momma *was* here when we were babies."

"It ain't got nothin' to do with the way things is, Missy. It's the way you sees them." Pepper sighed heavily, bent down and took a crock from under the sink. "She's a deep one, that Kate. Never know what she's up to. Now, you! You was an open book. Always knew jest from lookin' at you when you was about to git into some kind of mischief.

"And, by the by, if you reachin' for what I think you reachin' for, you jest do it up in the sunroom or someplace else, but not here in my kitchen."

Susannah managed a small embarrassed laugh and pulled an empty hand out of her jumper pocket. "What difference does it make?" she asked. "You know I smoke. What does it matter if I do it in front of you?"

Pepper sniffed. "I reckon you got a whole lot of bad habits, probably some fancy new ones, but I don't have to look at 'em." She turned away, and her body slumped as if she had let loose of her bones and muscles. She set the crock on the counter and extended her palms upward. "I swear, Susannah!" she cried. "What's to become of us? Lizbeth's drunk herself right into the grave, that youngun Page filled up with the same kind of poison that eats away at his momma, Jason all closed up inside hisself, God knows why, half the time, and you—my baby—two times a divorcee."

She took a handkerchief from her apron pocket and dabbed at her eyes. "I don't know what's to become of us. It's like we ain't even a family no more. Jest a sorry bunch of folks with the same mailbox. I's glad Gideon ain't here to see it."

Closing the subject abruptly, she took up the spiritual where she had left it and bent over the ham, making neat slices across the clove-studded diamonds with sure, swift strokes.

Susannah came up softly behind Pepper, putting her arms around her waist, leaning her cheek against her back. "Pepper? Please don't be mad at me."

Pepper put down the knife, turned quickly and hugged Susannah to her. "Darlin', I ain't mad at you. I gits exasperated sometimes, but that's jest 'cause I cares for you. I wants life to be good to you."

It seemed a good time, Susannah thought, to issue the standard invitation even though she knew it would receive the standard refusal after she had offered up all of her new and inventive reasons for why it was such a grand idea.

"I don't suppose it would do any good to ask you?"

Pepper turned her attention back to the ham. "To come to California with you?"

"Yes. A little later on when things are back to normal."

"No, wouldn't do no good."

"Not even to visit?"

"Did you git them peaches?"

Susannah started for the pantry, speaking over her shoulder. "It could mean a whole new life for you, Pepper. I'd send you to school if you'd like that. You know, a lot of older women are going back to school these days." She pretended not to notice Pepper, eyes cast up toward the ceiling as if calling on outside help, and went on enthusiastically. "Why you could learn to be a chef—a real chef and have your own little restaurant. Or, you're so good with hair, you could go to beauty school or someplace like that—you know, learn a trade."

"I got a trade."

"I mean something with a future where you could be your own woman."

"I am."

"Oh, Pepper! I mean something with dignity where maybe you could have a business of your own, have something for yourself."

"I don't figger the sort of work a body does takes 'way from his dignity, long as it's honest and somethin' a body's not 'shamed of."

"And just what, would you tell me, is dignified about cleaning other people's toilets?"

Pepper heaved a long sigh and chuckled deep in her throat. "Oh, you are still one to stir things up, now, ain't-cha? It sound to me like you been out there marchin' up and down with your black brothers."

Susannah drew herself up. "And what if I have? What's wrong with that?"

Pepper held her hands up in front of her. "Nuthin'! Nuthin' a tall. I jest hope you don't git your head bashed in runnin' around mindin' other folks business."

Susannah stuttered in agitation. "It's—it's everybody's business. Important things are happening in the world—"

Pepper interrupted her with mock seriousness. "I have noticed that very thing myself. You know, Missy, we do git three stations here in the woods on our TV, and of course we've had the radio for jest years now. Then they's the papers—the Martinsville paper keeps up with things pretty good, and we gits the Tulsa paper in the mail. They's Republican an' I don't hold much with the editorials, but news is news. And most folks here in Robina—includin' me—can read."

The thought entered Susannah's head that she should quit while she was only a little behind. But the truth of the matter was, she admitted to herself, losing was worth the pleasure of this old familiar banter. "What I meant," she said, "is that your people are fighting for their equality."

Pepper didn't miss a beat. "Why, it musta slipped your mind, Missy. Old King Solomon was my great-great-granddaddy. I don' wanna be equal with no common, ordinary white trash. Fact a business there's a lot of black trash I don' wanna be equal with, neither." Then she started a giggle that grew into a deep, musical laugh. "You so silly, Susannah! Why don' you leave off with all this rabble-rousin' and find youself a good sweet man and settle down and have some nice little kids? *Then* I might come out to California and take care of them kids and love 'em and paddle their britches when they need it." She laughed again and lifted her eyebrows with a sudden thought. "Why, I might even figure out some dignified way to clean your toilet."

Susannah drew back, clearly annoyed. "Why is it that everybody thinks a husband and a houseful of kids solves everything? There are more important things to be done in the world than populating it." She was speaking in her clear, bland television voice, hitting the consonants, hardening up the vowels that had started to slip away into a lazy drawl. "People are going to jail, Pepper, every day, to make it possible for your people to vote, to be educated, to have decent housing, to live like human beings. And you're treating it like some kind of joke."

Pepper's laughter stopped, her face became a smooth mask, and she stared at Susannah for a long, breathless moment before she spoke. "No, it ain't no joke. I's laughin' at you. Don' think I ain't been keepin' track of your foolishness. Fact a business, lately, ever' time you on the television, I prays the Lord to send a great power failure to Robina County."

Susannah gazed studiously at her feet, thinking woefully of some of the grubby frogs and toads that had hopped out of her mouth in living color.

But Pepper's huff had not run its course. "I knows a little somethin' about this problem," she said indignantly. "I ain't jest been standin' around gawkin' at my life, I been livin' in it for sixty years. I tell you, if it ain't the bigots it's the bleedin' hearts! I'm put to mind of one time I went to Tulsa to do me some Christmas shoppin'. This little snip of a girl with her big eyes so full of charity they could pick your pockets, she got on the bus jest before me and she turns and smiles at me in kind of a sad way. You could see she was jest bubblin' over with goodwill and lookin' for somebody to do a good deed to. Well, she plops herself down there in the last seat in the back, there in the colored folks' section. I says politely that they's seats for her up front. She looks at me outa them charitable eyes and says I's to have her seat and she'll take mine. And she sat there in all her lovin' kindness while I stands up on my poor old sore feet all the way to Greenwood Avenue."

"Now, wait just a minute, Pepper—"

"No, you wait, Miss Smarty-Drawers! When I come to work here nobody 'round these parts ever heard of civil rights or equal opportunity. That first day, I says to your granddaddy, I says, 'Mister Warwick, suh, where would you like to take your coffee?' And he says right back that since he figgered on callin' me Pepper if it was okay by me, then I was to call him Gideon, on 'counta he never used a first name on no grownup that didn't use his back. That was my first experience at bein' equal, an' I ain't never goin' to forget it.

"He was God's man, and I knows in my heart they's others like him, but I seen too many with sugar in one hand and a stick in the other. And some of them fellers that's supposed to be lookin' after the black folks' interests, why, any fool can see it's like sendin' a fox to watch over the henhouse."

"Pepper, I—"

"I ain't done yet. Put some marshmallows on top them sweet potatoes and set 'em by the stove." She closed her eyes and tilted her head thoughtfully. "When came time for my little Esau to go for his schoolin', Gideon didn't give folks a chance to use us for they own problems. No suh! He says, 'Now, this boy's got to go to school and we ain't got but the one, an' that's where he's goin'.' And when he sent him on to Langston and then to Harvard University in Boston, Massachusetts, he took it outa my pay and outa my profits off my investments so's I's the one that done it."

She paused and drew herself up proudly. "I was the first

one in my family to go to school. Finished all the way through the sixth grade. Now I's sent my boy through college and lawyer's school—"

"Investments?"

"My investments in Gideon's beef cattle," she answered. "Here I got more'n forty thousand dollars in the savin' and loan in Martinsville, gits a nice little check ever' month, and you wants to send me to beauty school so's I can learn hair straighten' and be my own woman."

"But—but," Susannah sputtered, "if you have an income why are you here? Why are you working?"

Pepper handed Susannah the ham-filled platter. "I tell you it's like sunshine after a week of gray days havin' you home to fuss with. I'm workin' 'cause this is my job. I'm here 'cause this is my home. Oh, come on, now, Missy, don' be a sore loser. You can eat a few words now an' agin—they ain't fattenin'. You start gettin' these things on the table now and I'll see to the pies."

Susannah had just covered the last dish with Saran Wrap when loud barking announced the first caller.

"You git it, honey," Pepper called from the kitchen.

Susannah looked through one of the beveled-glass panes that flanked the front door and frowned at the black derby and turned collar. She opened the door and said coolly, "How do you do, I'm Mrs. Garrity's sister, Susannah Sullivan."

"I'm Father Flesher," the priest said as she took his hat and led him into the hall. He smiled. "I'm familiar with some of your—your work."

"I'm sure you are," Susannah replied with a knowing smile. "Won't you come in the living room. Could I get you some coffee? Sherry?"

"Sherry would be fine—fine, thank you. I'm very sorry about your mother. I know it must have been a shock to you."

She tilted her head with the expression of one who is about to clear up matters, to set things straight. "Thank you, Father, but my mother and I were never close, we hardly knew each other. Frankly, I'm shocked that she didn't die of an outraged liver years ago." Immediately, she regretted her words and could almost feel Gran's presence fill the room. *There's no call for that kind of talk* . . .

Father Flesher walked to the fireplace, rubbed his hands together and held them out to the fire. He spoke musingly. "Life, as we know it, is always fatal, Miss Sullivan. It is unfortunate, however, if it causes bitterness rather than sadness in those who are left behind."

She placed the silver tray with its Waterford glasses and matching decanter in front of him on the coffee table and filled one glass with sherry. "Father," she said softly, "I've just gotten one dressing down I suspect I richly deserved, and I guess I'm still smarting from it." She smiled and held out the glass. "Please forgive my rudeness. Excuse me, I'll get Kate."

She hurried up the stairs and knocked lightly on Kate's door.

"Yes?"

"He's here. May I come in?" She opened the door a crack to see Kate stretched across one of the twin beds, a wash-cloth over her eyes. "Headache?"

"I think I'm holding off a migraine. Did you talk to him?"

Susannah grimaced. "Just long enough to demonstrate my famous hoof-in-mouth trick." She crossed to the windows, pushed the white priscillas to one side and looked out. "I think I'll see if Marty and Hodge are going to ride out for a while. I've got a bad case of the disagreeables. You mind?"

Kate slipped her feet into the shoes beside the bed. "Not at all. As a matter of fact, I'm rather relieved."

Susannah noted but did not respond to her sister's mild sarcasm. "Sure you don't mind?" she insisted. "Page said something about—"

"Oh, don't pay any attention to Page. That boy is diffi-cult about everything lately—a phase, I guess." Kate walked heavily toward the door, then turned. "Is there anything in particular you'd like Father Flesher to say? Or to read from?"

Susannah dropped the curtain. "How about—

> 'Indeed the idols I have loved so long
> Have done my credit in the World much wrong
> Have drown'd my Glory in a shallow cup
> And sold my reputation for a song.'"

Kate met Susannah's innocent gaze and held it for a long moment before she left the room. Susannah shrugged, hurried to her own room and changed into jeans, boots and a heavy sweater. She took an old mackinaw from the closet and threw it over her shoulders.

At the other end of the hall, Marty, also in Levi's and boots, answered her knock.

"Wow! Do you look spiffy!" she exclaimed.

"A loan from the Marlboro Man."

"Who?"

"Your brother-in-law."

She looked at him blankly. She had never thought of Jason in quite those terms. He was married to her sister, yes. He was Kate's husband and the father of her children. But she had never thought of him as a—a relative?

"You going with us?" he asked.

She nodded. "The local mourners are about to descend upon us, and the idea of being neighborly gives me the drearies."

"Aren't there some old friends you'd like to see?"

"Yeah," she said wryly. "Round about the year two thousand would be just dandy. I had more than enough homecoming the last time I was here, thank you. Where's Hodge?"

"Gone to ask Pepper to pack us a snack for our trek."

"You met her yet?"

"No. Hodge said after we get back. Said she doesn't like people underfoot in her kitchen when she's cooking." He motioned to a leather case on the sewing machine. "Want a drink?"

She opened her eyes wide. "What a splendid idea!"

He flipped the latch on the bag. Inside were heavy silver

flasks, monogrammed with mother-of-pearl. "Scotch or vodka?"

"Anything but sherry."

"So," he said, pouring scotch into the bright-rimmed glasses, "what happened at your last homecoming?"

She took the glass, sat down on the brass bed, leaned back on the pillows and closed her eyes. "Ah yes, now I see them—marching six abreast across my memory. Marylouise wanted to give me a party. Marylouise—gorgeous oil-rich old maid. Old maid by Robina standards, that is— any female over twenty-five years old who hasn't married. Old maids and grass widows are frowned upon, but, like I said, she's rich, and that means the same thing in Robina as it does anyplace else in the world.

"Well, Marylouise was my best friend." She paused thoughtfully. "That's not quite true. She was my best friend when she wasn't being Kate's best friend. She sailed back and forth between us like a Ping-Pong ball, and Kate and I would have these unbelievable knock-down-drag-outs because of it."

Her features softened, and she smiled dreamily. "Young girls, you know. . ." She looked at him apologetically. "No, I guess you don't know. Boys aren't allowed this kind of thing. But girls, they have such grand crushes on each other, full of drama and ecstasy and pledges of undying loyalty. It's an erotic experience, not necessarily homosexual, I mean in the strictest sense. Oh, there may be some experimental rubbing around here and there, but usually nothing full-blown." She looked up at him and smiled playfully. "So to speak.

"Well, Marylouise and I had this *thing*. And oh such a wonderful, innocent thing it was! She had read someplace that sucking on breasts made them bigger. We were thirteen apiece, flat as old pine boards and bilious green from the neck up 'cause Gran had hauled Kate off to Martinsville to buy her a bra." She frowned and was thoughtful. "We called them brassieres then, remember? Maybe that's why people are burning them.

"Anyway, Kate was a year older, so it was natural, but

we didn't think about that. Obviously, we had to do something to catch up, we couldn't reach the little buggers ourselves, so the solution was to accommodate each other. We had to do something! The way we saw it—which was not the way it was, of course—was Kate parading around with her shoulderblades damn near fused behind, showing off these little pointed wonders on her chest and by God they were getting fatter and rounder and more wonderful by the hour.

"So we decided to do it. Every day for a week we troop off to the storm cellar for a treatment. At the end of the week we get out the tape measure and here we are—after all that discipline, all that hard, sweaty work—still flat as boards, still bilious green with envy. So, we decide to give that up, and we send off for a breast developer that Marylouise finds advertised in a movie magazine, results guaranteed, comes in a plain brown wrapper."

Marty was laughing now, out loud, and Susannah started to laugh, too, laughed until tears came to her eyes. "Oh, God," she gasped. "Oh, God, growing up is so painful."

She wiped her eyes and cleared her throat with an air of getting back to the matter at hand. "Anyway, sex or attraction or whatever it is, is a part of it, but the special thing is being best friends—talkingtalkingtalkingTALKING! When you're not together you're on the telephone, you're wearing each other's clothes. . ." Her words trailed off and she held her glass out for a refill. "Blair was always so pissed because I wore his shirts. He didn't understand I was just trying to be his friend . . . Where was I?"

"Talking on the phone and wearing each other's duds."

"Right. Inseparable, born brand-new in each other every day and always the talking. Sharing your deepest thoughts, your darkest most unspeakable secrets." She looked up, took the glass that he handed her and gave out a great long sigh. "Then it's over for one reason or another—a boy, a blouse that wasn't returned, you got an A and she got a B, something, anything, and it's awful! After a siege of melancholy you stir yourself and find another eternal friendship, swearing the same vows. Ah, but the rub is, this time

telling not only your own unspeakables, but also those entrusted to your care. As you can imagine, with this Ping-
Pong effect we had going, Kate and I really got the goods
on each other."

"Did Kate and Marylouise . . .?"

"You kidding? Saint Catherine? I bet you think she made
all those kids the usual way. Wrong! The stork brought
them—only documented case in human history."

Marty chuckled and said, "You were telling me about the
homecoming?"

"Ah yes, I do digress. Well, Marylouise gives this tea in
my honor—high tea, my dear, with the silver service and
the bone china cups." She fluttered her eyelids and lifted
one shoulder to her chin. "'You must let me do this, Susannah, darlin'! You can't deny me this pleasure, and we're
alllll soooo proud of you.'

"Well, I knew better than that, but I went, draggin' ass,
with Pepper hollering at me from the front porch not to
disgrace the family. All the ladies were there, even the
society editor from Martinsville. It starts out innocently
enough—they want to know if it's true what they read in
the movie magazines at the beauty parlor. The usual—
who's committing adultery with who, who's gay, who's
had a facelift, and do they, is it really true, do they, tisk
tisk, have some of their other parts lifted, too? For some
reason still unknown to me I elected myself as some kind of
public-relations outfit, and I allowed as how there were
folks in southern California who went to church on Sunday, who worried about their kids' grades, supported the
local library and even voted a straight Republican ticket.

"That went over like little mouse turds in the punch
bowl. So, the good ladies got on my case about my poor
frazzled marital history and my shocking lack of offspring
at my advanced age. But they did it in this polite, mincy-
footed way so I couldn't get a good hold on anything to toss
back. It was like being paralyzed by civility, you know
what I mean?" Marty nodded sympathetically. She looked
directly at him, her head tilted, her expression sad and
puzzled. "Kate didn't help me—you know? I was Mary-

louise's entertainment for the day. The two of them just floated around and smiled and nodded and let it all go by. The old triangle was still in place, with me all by myself out there on the point."

Marty nodded again like someone who has the ways of the world under surveillance, who was no longer surprised by anything. "Speaking of which," he said. "Your frayed marital history, that is. Hodge asked me if I'm going to be your next husband."

"Oh? What did you say?"

"I told him that we're business associates and that it isn't the best setup for a long and happy union. He really tried to sell me on it. Said you could cut yearlings out of a running herd, skin a rabbit, bait a fishhook. . ." Susannah giggled and puffed out her chest. "He said," Marty continued in mock seriousness, "that he figured it was probably not easy to find a girl you like well enough to live with, that most of them were pretty silly and couldn't do anything practical. I assume he means practical things like skinning rabbits. *Then* he said, and I had some trouble keeping a straight face on this one, he said that Pepper said—Susannah, I can hardly wait to meet that woman—"

"Come on, come on, Marty, what?"

"Pepper said, according to Hodge, that the way you know for certain that it's true love is if you can answer yes to the question 'Do I want to be buried next to this person?'" His world-weary smile had faded midsentence, and his face was quite straight. "Come to think of it," he said, sounding somewhat bewildered, "I guess that's not such a funny question after all."

Susannah looked thoughtful. "Did you, Marty?"

"Did I what?"

"Ever think about committing holy matrimony with me?"

He nodded. "Once. Yeah, I thought about it once."

"When was that?"

"A hundred years ago—on Santa Monica Boulevard. We were at the Laundromat."

"That's funny. I don't remember any great moments doing the laundry."

"We were on our way to dinner, and you had to stop and pick up your stuff which you would leave in the dryer and God would protect. There was nobody else there but this little old lady. She was having trouble making the machine go and you asked if you could help her."

Susannah's face brightened. "Sure! I remember! The old woman with the fantastic face, like the Russian, Anna What's-er-name . . ."

"Marie What's-er-name. After you showed her what to do, she asked you if you worked there."

"I don't remember that."

"I do. You grinned like some kind of loony and you hugged her and you told her you worked in the world. Then *she* grins and the two of you do this little jig around the washing machines."

"That turned you on?"

"Set fire to my very cockles." He reached down and patted her head. "I've always been drawn to m'shugena women."

"But you didn't ask."

"No. But we made love all night even unto the next day. Verily."

"Why didn't you ask?" Susannah insisted.

Marty looked uncomfortable. He was deeper into this conversation than he wanted to be, and his attempts to lift it back to safe ground were not working. He sighed. "It wasn't enough. It was great for what it was—Jesus, that weekend is enshrined forever in my hall of records."

"Marty?"

He sighed again. "Okay. I guess I'm just old-fashioned, Susannah. I know that's not easy to believe. But if a man and a woman consider something as *impossible* as marriage— I mean, given the odds—then they should at the very least be in love with each other."

"I love you, Marty," she said simply.

He ran his hand through his hair, and spoke in a halting

manner. "I know, I know, I believe that. You love me, yes, like your old sneakers."

She shook her head softly from side to side. "It's more than that, much more. And I need you, Marty."

"What you need you get from the agent and the friend and the man you sometimes call up when your bed's too empty and things go bump in the night. I want more out of a marriage than that."

"Like what?"

"Don't laugh—"

"Do I look like somebody who's about to laugh?"

"Well, it sounds corny, but I want somebody to hear bells when I look at her, when I touch her. Did I ever ring any bells for you, Susannah?"

She was silent. He had, of course, in the beginning, but she had been too absorbed in tolling the harsh and clanging memory of Jason to hear. Anyway, that was a long time ago. "I don't do bells, Marty," she said lightly. "Not anymore. I stood too close once and got knocked in the head on the backward swing." She leaned toward him. "Lots of people do it, good friends get married and manage very well without the grand passion."

"That's not a marriage. That's having somebody around to witness your heart attack." He looked at her for a long time, then said quietly, "I don't know if this is a proposal or not. I'm honored if it is, but I guess the truth of the matter is that I don't do bells anymore, either."

There was a hush in the air. Marty wondered if he had spoken the truth or if instead he had caused something to become true because it had been spoken. "Wait!" he said suddenly. "Don't commit that to memory. I don't know if that's what I really think."

Susannah smiled broadly, swung her legs over the side of the bed and started toward him, then they both turned at the sound of the stairs being taken two at a time.

Hodge came through the door carrying an old wicker picnic basket. "Pepper made us a bitchin' lunch," he said cheerfully. "You going with us, Susannah?"

She was staring at the basket, the one she had packed and carried to the creek day after day that long summer.

"Susannah?" Hodge repeated, peering into her face.

"Oh yes, I'm sorry. Yes. Where're you going?"

"I thought we'd ride out through the north pasture and see the herd, then we could head down to the bottom and have our lunch in the shack."

"The shack?"

"Jason's old place. You know."

"Yes, I know. How 'bout if we have lunch at the spring. Is the lean-to still there?"

"It's there. Sure, we can do that."

"Is Page going? Did you ask him?"

"I asked him all right. But he said it's disrespectful to have fun till after the funeral tomorrow." He lifted his shoulders in a gesture of puzzlement. "Thing is, I don't know where he got this respect all of a sudden." He shook his head and handed the basket to Marty. "I got to make a stop at the storm cellar. Pepper needs some watermelon pickles. You all want to meet me in the stables?"

"I'd like to see the storm cellar," said Marty. He looked at Susannah from the corner of his eye and added, "I've heard a lot about it."

They moved quietly down the stairs, tiptoed past the low voices that came from the living room, and went out by way of the back hall. From the porch the snow glistened in the pale winter sun; the air was crisp and still and filled with the smell of wood smoke. Hodge led the way several yards beyond the east side of the house, bent down and brushed snow from around a large iron ring, pulled open the heavy door, then disappeared down a steep bank of narrow stairs.

"Wait till I light the lantern," he called from below. Then a moment later, "Okay, watch your step."

Inside, Marty let out a low whistle as he looked around him. "I thought storm cellars were dusty and full of cobwebs and ghosts."

Hodge passed his hand over a long row of Mason jars and

held it up for Marty's inspection. "Things that belong to my mom are not allowed to get dusty. I expect there're some ghosts here, though."

Slowly, Marty's eyes traveled around the room. And it *was* a room, not just a hole in the ground: its four walls lined with shelves of canned fruit and vegetables, sleeping ledges hacked out of earth and rock and covered with feather pads, an assortment of lanterns, a Coleman stove, water jugs, a radio, paperback books, a first-aid kit hanging by the stairs, a cribbage board, a Monopoly set, and, in the center of it all, a long pipe extending from above.

"Grampa built that," Susannah said. "It's a combination air hole and periscope."

Marty shook his head in wonder. "It looks like you're ready for a siege."

"We are," Hodge said, laughing. "Gideon didn't leave anything to chance. Here, see. . ." He pulled a chest away from the wall under the stairs to reveal a dark hole, crouch height. "This goes into the woods."

"What for?" Marty asked.

"In case of a cave-in," Susannah answered. "Like Hodge says, Grampa didn't leave anything to chance."

Hodge reached to a top shelf and brought down a quart jar of pickles. "You guys ready?"

Marty lingered, still taking in the room, as Hodge and Susannah started up the stairs. "You don't have to wait for a storm," Hodge offered. "You can spend the night here if you want to. I did lots of times when I was young. I'd sneak out through the tunnel and meet some of the guys and we'd play robbers and ghosts and things like that."

Marty came quickly up the stairs. "Thanks, Hodge," he said with a show of politeness. "Thanks just the same, but I'm very comfortable in the sunroom."

Hodge dashed off to deliver the pickles, then caught up with Marty and Susannah on the path to the stables, where he veered off suddenly toward the barn. "I want to show you something," he said, motioning for them to follow. "It'll only take a minute."

It was dim and gray inside, with thin lines of light falling through the cracks from the loft; the air was cool but not cold, heavy with the smell of hay and manure. They followed him the length of the barn to a large fenced-off area in the rear: chain-link, silver-new and out of place, with posts for reinforcement every four feet or so, a fence that meant business.

"They're a little skittish," Hodge said softly. "Best not to make any sudden movements."

For the second time, in response to the wonders of the Garrity Ranch, Marty let out a low whistle. "Son of a bitch!" he said under his breath.

"My God," Susannah whispered, "it's some kind of elephant."

There were two of them, one considerably larger than the other; that one, the male, at least six feet tall at the shoulder and almost twice that in length, with a heavy bisonlike hump on its neck and back, and loose velvety dewlaps that hung beneath the chin and between the forelegs. The short-haired, pitch-black coat shone even in the muted light like that of a just-groomed Doberman. The smaller one, the female, was a rich russet color, and both had white stockings that came halfway up their curiously delicate-looking legs. The muzzles were a wet shiny white, the eyes wide-set with an Oriental slant, the hair on the top of the head frosted at the tips, and from the sides horns curved out and upward: massive and corrugated and olive drab on the bull; thinner, smooth and dun-colored on the cow.

Both animals, showing the whites around their dark eyes, stared suspiciously at their visitors, then suddenly the bull lifted his head, the muzzle high, his long tail whipping back and forth. He jabbed the air with one horn, then swung his head and forequarters from side to side, giving off short snorts that ended in a hoarse bellow.

Susannah jumped back, quickly followed by both Marty and Hodge. The bull jabbed the air again in their direction, blew out through his nose, then circled the pen in stiff-legged bounds.

"What is it?" Susannah murmured, still inching backward.

"Gaur," Hodge answered. "It's okay, they can't get out."

But his words did not carry enough assurance to suit Susannah. She took short sideways steps toward the barn's entrance, and was soon after joined by Marty and Hodge. Outside, she took a deep breath and spread one hand over her chest.

"Awesome," she said. "What did you call them?"

He spelled it, "g-a-u-r," and went on instructively, "The largest of the wild cattle. They've never been hybridized successfully in this country. Jason wants to breed them to his Sanlanders."

"What on earth *for*?"

Hodge laughed. "What else? Beef."

Susannah shook her head decisively. "It'll never work. That thing back there would scare the beejesus out of a lady Sanlander."

Once again, they started toward the stables, and Hodge told them of how Jason had made a deal with the director of the zoo in Oklahoma City. He had this pair on a kind of breeding loan in return for financing a new giraffe barn at the zoo. With this gaur, this giant bovid that would eat anything, that resisted disease and domestication with equal vigor, that even the great tigers in the forests of its home in India wanted no part of, Jason hoped to produce a new strain that would yield yet more dressed beef per animal, yet more blue ribbons per state fair.

Susannah nodded and smiled a little. "Bigger and better bulls, huh?" she said, her voice heavy with irony.

"What?" Hodge leaned toward her, and Marty narrowed his eyes with a look that said Careful There.

Susannah cleared her throat. Of course Marty was right. One did not heap sarcasm about the father onto the innocent head of the son. "I was just thinking," she said, hoping to sound offhand, "that your dad has always had this interest, this fascination with large bulls."

"You think it's Freudian or something like that?" Hodge asked.

Susannah's head came around. Were they delivering up the study of sex symbols in elementary school these days?

He grinned at her like someone sharing a dirty joke, but his face was flushed. "I don't know exactly what that means, but that's what Mom said when he got them. She was—well, she was mad at him." Then he added hesitantly, as if he had already said more than he intended, "For being gone so much, I think."

Inside, washing through like well-swirled brandy, Susannah felt a kind of elation. Well, well, what do we have here? Serves old tightass right. Then she immediately chastised herself, but mildly, just enough to feel virtuous. "Well," she said, beaming well-lit approval on both of them, "are we going to ride horses today or not?"

Inside the stables, Hodge handed out brushes, bridles, saddle blankets, saddles, and said to Susannah, with the reverence with which a gift saved up for a long time is offered, "Would you like to ride The Sullivan?"

She looked at him for a long grateful moment, then crossed to where he stood, bridle dangling from his hand, and kissed him on the cheek. "Thank you, Hodge. I'd like that very much." She took the bridle and approached the first stall. The horse whinnied softly, and Susannah whinnied back from deep in her throat. "Spittin' image, right?" she said to Hodge. "I mean the markings." And to Marty, "Isn't she beautiful!" She gestured as if introducing the guest of honor. "This," she said grandly, "is Bright Feather's only child. Bright Feather was my horse—my Appaloosa. They wouldn't breed her because they thought she was crazy and *everybody* knows that craziness is passed down through the females. But she fooled them, she just hied herself off down the road one warm evening and seduced one of Marylouise's Arabs. Just look! She's Bright Feather all over again, with the Arab's head. Come on. Oh! Let's go."

Susannah rode behind them, not with them at all, but caught in a time warp where she was astride not this horse, but its mother. She could hear their voices floating back to her, but they were miles and years away. The present was a slippery item to keep a good hold on, especially here with the past so intrusive.

It was "*gaur*," Hodge was telling Marty, just plain "gaur" whether you were talking about one or a dozen.

"*Gertrudis*" Jason had said, the same for the singular or plural. *That* one, that most singular of all bulls, did it survive? No one wrote to tell her one way or the other. She hadn't asked. No way. It just ceased to exist, the issue of destruction, the cause of it all, and she never knew if it lived or died.

Hodge was hollering at her to look off to the right, to look down on the herd. Maybe the bastard *had* lived and had sired the sires of all those little dots down there in the valley. A dynasty of New York steaks; succulent rump roasts squatting in the middle of pinkish new potatoes and baby carrots; prime rib dribbling blood into the Yorkshire pudding. That poor sad wild black monster in the barn back there was to be the father of a good thick stew. Castrated beef, marbled by a passive asexual life—only the fittest left intact.

Mountain oysters.

When Gideon was away, the ranch hands would flip pennies for the balls they sliced off the calves. Afterward, fry them up with scrambled eggs. One of the men, old Jules, would pop them into his toothless mouth right on the spot and, with his hand lightly caressing his body, would pretend to follow their progress down his gullet into his stomach, then through his gut. Then he would grin savagely, showing his pink gums, rolling his watery blue eyes, as a bulge appeared in the crotch of his jeans. This ritual took place only when Gideon was away from the ranch. When he was there, in attendance, his pocketknife sharpened to a glittering edge on the whetstone, the oysters went into a red bucket and later, for some reason Susannah never understood, were given a decent burial. Deeply mourned by the hands. Especially old Jules.

Now Marty was back on the gaur. He wanted to know why they interbred with the cattle in their own country but not here. Hodge didn't know. He thought it might have something to do with their being wild animals in a captive situation. That's what Jason said. Maybe they'd have to use artificial insemination.

The History of the World by artificial insemination: Jason pumping in Spengler and Spencer, Susannah unfaithful to Literature 101. Brain fertile as a brood sow, ovulated three-four times a day that spring and summer, sperm slithered through gray matter in pursuit of egg—bingo! (Bull's eye?) Gave birth to many lies about life.

Got heart pregnant, too—false labor of love. And soul. Not body. Very careful about body. Careless with Heart and Soul, not necessary to take them to Kansas City for abortion. Now have hysterectomy of heart, can't get knocked up anymore. But oh! All those little souls still running about. All those orphan hopes . . .

"What?"

Hodge was asking her something. Did she want to get closer to the herd? No, she didn't. Should they go on over to the spring and have lunch? Yes, that would be fine. Was she okay, Marty wanted to know. Yes, just fine. Just enjoying the ride. And wallowing, she admitted to herself.

They turned south and rode along the edge of the duck pond. Now Marty was answering Hodge's questions about himself. He was answering straight out and earnest, not pulling back or making jokes. His great-grandparents came from Glasgow. His great-grandfather was a painter and they came because the opportunities for an artist were better in the United States.

She didn't know *that*. Why didn't she know that? She thought they'd come from Poland or Russia during a pogrom, fleeing for their lives.

Who ever heard of a Jew from Scotland? For years now she'd had this nice neat picture of Marty's heritage. A grandfather with the long curls in front of his ears, sitting at the cluttered kitchen table, reading from the Torah and drinking hot tea from a glass with a spoon in it. A short round grandmother who went out every day into the streets with her string bag to buy vegetables and haggle with the butcher for a soup bone. She didn't see his parents so clearly. Third generations had a way of becoming ordinary, with no exotic habits or string bags to distinguish them.

Hodge called back to say he was going on ahead to make a fire at the lean-to, and Susannah urged her horse forward to join Marty.

"What did he paint?" she asked.

"My great-grandfather? Oils. Portraits, mostly, for a living, and he did some nice seascapes. There's one in the Metropolitan."

She looked miffed. "I didn't know that." It was disconcerting when people brought in their own pictures to replace those you had been obliged to draw out of skimpy information. "Why didn't you tell me?" she asked peevishly.

"You didn't ask."

"I did too! You know I did! And 'cause you're so goddamn stingy with yourself I've had to make up this big story about pogroms and pushcarts and you leaving home because they wanted you to be a rabbi."

Marty threw his head back and laughed. "So far as I know we've never been run out of anyplace. Uh, wait—the dining room in the Brown Palace in Denver one time, but that was because I didn't have a tie." He glanced over at her in amusement. "I'm sorry to spoil the cliché for you, but the truth of the matter is that nobody has lit any Friday-night candles for over two hundred years. My great-grandfather thought of himself as a Scot. My grandfather, my dad saw themselves as Americans. Me? I'm a Californian. I believe—devoutly—in mild climates."

"Marty! Be serious!"

"Come on, Susannah. What's the point of reaching way back into history to become someone you're not? I don't want to go to Israel, live in a kibbutz and get my ass shot at any more than you want to go to Ireland and raise potatoes and get your ass shot at." He raised his shoulders, opened his palms, and tilted his head far to one side, pulling a hopeless face. "I've never even been to a seder. And my command of the language is limited to *shiksa* and *m'shugana* and what do you want from me."

"I can assure you," Susannah said gravely, "if there had been six million Irishmen burned up in ovens, I'd feel a kinship with the survivors." She had formed the words earnestly, but somehow, even to her own ears, they had a hollow, self-satisfied ring.

His expression changed and he was, as she had requested, quite serious. "That one belongs to everybody, Susannah. You don't have to be Jewish to be outraged." Then he sat up very straight and shielded his eyes to look off into the distance. "Hey, look! I think I see smoke from yonder campfire."

Susannah smiled at him, reflecting on the many sides of Martin Stone, thinking about how long it took to get to know the people you knew well.

She let out a whoop and kicked The Sullivan into a lope. "Race you!" she cried.

He kicked his own horse and closed the gap between them. "Susannah?" he called to her.

"WHAT?"

"You didn't tell me. What was in the package you sent for?"

"What package?"

"The breast developer in the plain brown wrapper?"

"A HAND!" she yelled over her shoulder. "A RUBBER HAND!"

NINE

SUSANNAH SAT as she had been taught as a child, hands folded in her lap, back straight, legs crossed at the ankles. She wore a severe but elegant three-piece suit of fine black worsted, a white silk blouse, and a velvet cloche.

"You better put somethin' else on your feet," Pepper said, eyeing the open-toed shoes. "You'll catch your death."

"Isn't it time for the car?" Susannah asked listlessly. "Where's Kate?"

"She's gettin' herself ready. We got plenty of time yet. You better take that coat off, you'll be cold when you gits outdoors."

"Pepper, please! I'm thirty-two years old, will you stop clucking at me."

"You thirty-four in October, Missy," Pepper retorted, turning away. She took a straw sailor from the mantel and centered it carefully on her head, fixing it with a ruby hat pin. She wore her Sunday dress, a dark-blue woolen with white lace collar and cuffs; her heavy reddish cotton hose; her good shoes—those that hadn't yet been cut with a razor blade where they pinched her toes.

"We missed you last evenin'," she said. "You all right? Ain't like you to go off to bed 'fore suppertime."

"I was tired, we had a long ride."

"I had a nice talk with your friend, he seems a real good sort."

"Did you tell him I can bait a hook?" Pepper looked puzzled. "Hodge asked Marty if he was going to marry me," Susannah explained. "Told him I could do a lot of useful things like putting worms on hooks. It broke Marty up."

Pepper rubbed her chin and continued to look puzzled. "Somethin' about that man," she said slowly. "He's got a deep hurt in him."

"Marty?" Susannah shrugged. "His wife died unexpectedly. But that was a *long* time ago."

Pepper nodded her head, satisfied.

"It was a long time ago," Susannah repeated.

"That don't matter," Pepper said. "We don't live long enough for anything that happens to us to be a *long* time ago. Anyway, he seems a good man. You could do a lot worse. Even the animals likes him. That's a sure sign of good character, when the animals takes to a stranger. He helped Patrick feed the dogs, and when he and me was visitin' after supper old Iago got up in his lap. An' you know that cat won't take up with hardly nobody."

"That's certainly an impressive recommendation," Susannah said loftily. "On the strength of Iago's wisdom and insight, I'll take the matter under advisement."

Pepper was pulling on her gloves, watching Susannah closely. "Missy," she said, "what is it makes you that way?"

"What way?"

"Always play-actin', pretendin' the things that matter don't matter?"

"Oh, Pepper. . ."

"How come you marryin' so much anyhow? Cain't you keep holt of a man?"

Susannah looked straight up at the ceiling. "Things are different in California," she said with exaggerated patience.

Pepper snorted. "Things may be different, but men is the same all over. None of 'em really wants to stay married. You gotta keep convincin' them that they likes it. Now, what was wrong with that first feller? I watched him on the television and he was right nice to look at. Fact a business, he's near a dead ringer for Jason."

"You really think so? I never noticed."

Now it was Pepper's turn to look at the ceiling.

Susannah gave an inch. "I suppose you *could* say there's a slight resemblance."

And she caught a glimpse of Wichita Cabot on the edge of her memory, saw the beautiful people in their benefit-tennis whites, saw the white tables with their white wrought-iron chairs and yellow umbrellas, saw the wide expanse of green dichondra surrounding the courts, saw herself, white on tan, as she moved across it from one huddle of players to another, gliding gracefully in ever smaller circles until she found herself facing him.

Same winter-wheat hair, same morning-glory eyes, and, it turned out, so unlike the macho cowboy he portrayed each week. His mind was a library of foreign cookbooks, vintage wines, librettos, zodiacal interpretations, cult movies, Jungian papers, and American poets. Really. Poetry.

Two weeks after their meeting on the dichondra they were married, and six months after that he fled from her in the fuzzy exhaustion of a man saved from drowning.

What do you mean you're leaving?

Just that, my dear. I, the subject; am, the verb; leaving, the participle; and lest it dangle, you, the object.

Location? Are you going on location?

I'm going to a hotel. I am leaving you before you kill me with kindness.

He pushed past her and dashed up the winding staircase. She stood for a moment in shocked silence, then went after him, gathering up the trailing hem of her clinging satin gown, one of her many costumes for the nightly entertainment she produced and directed. The martinis were in the refrigerator, a Caesar salad waited to be assembled, dressed and tossed, tenderloin *en brochette* marinated next to the broiler, a single rose bloomed from a silver bud vase in the center of a carefully set table, the fire crackled, and the record player sent selected sensuous strains throughout the house. Props and effects in readiness, it was time for the play to begin.

The door to their bedroom was closed. She brought her knuckles up to tap on it lightly—do not disturb disturbed people—then instead flung it open. The drawers in the Spanish highboy were pulled out; clothes were strewn across the bed, on the floor; suitcases were open, half filled. Chaos.

She spoke softly. Wich—let's sit down and let's talk about this. Let's talk about it reasonably—

There's nothing to talk about.

But—

I am sick of your reasons, Susannah, not to mention your patience, your deadly mercy and your wretched good heart. In that order.

She moved swiftly across the room and gathered a pile of socks and underwear from the heap on the bed, clutching them to her breast. Oh, darling, don't give up, she pleaded, you're getting better.

He snatched the socks and underwear away from her and dumped them into one of the suitcases. I am not getting better—I am dying.

But last night was a turning point, she insisted.

Last night I got it up and got it in that sacred cave. What does that prove?

Oh, Wich, and she sank down, a small, shiny bundle on the foot of the bed. What does the doctor say?

He says that you are in worse shape than I am.

That's not true!

Then why did you marry me if you're so frigging healthy?

I didn't know. I didn't know about your problem.

My problem. Laughter, peels of it. You married me so you wouldn't have to clutter up your life with nuptial fucking, but then your old fundamentalist God Almighty laid a hand on you and said thou shalt know this man and plant his seed.

She stood up and watched him as he tossed his cashmere sweaters, like so many mop rags, into a bag. Then she started for the door, trying for dignity, but her feet got tangled in the hem of her long skirt. She caught herself, whirled dramatically and told him: If you want to know the truth, I married you because you reminded me of someone else—a real man.

"Oh all right, Pepper! So he did remind me of Jason. At first. But he wasn't like Jason at all. Wichita didn't like women—I mean *that* way. He couldn't—well, you know what I mean."

Pepper clicked her tongue sympathetically. "What about the next one? What ailed him?"

Susannah managed a wan smile. "Oh, he liked women all right. Harems, scads, whole herds of them. All sizes, shapes and colors, right from the beginning."

And in the beginning, somehow she hadn't minded. The youthful, full-maned, big-titted creatures who swarmed around him were, she thought, harmless and simply part of the price one paid for such a marriage. The famous, near-famous and used-to-be-famous who peopled the gold-and-white penthouse high above the Sunset Strip were proof that her existence had glamor. They were, in a way, siblings of those tea-sipping specters who still haunted the many-gabled Hawthorne house of an earlier fantasy.

But gradually she realized that this was not some kind of extended honeymoon, that Blair's plans for the future did not, like hers, include a rambling old house in Brentwood and, most especially, the children to fill it.

I have no interest in people who are two feet tall, he said. Good heavens, Susannah, do you know what happens to people when they start *breeding?* They lose their identity. Their lives become one giant car pool. Grown-up, self-respecting men turn into monstrous things like Little League coaches and scoutmasters and pals forever.

Oh, that's nonsense, Blair. It doesn't have to be that way.

No. *No!* Not now. Perhaps later. I simply haven't the time right now to take up fathering. Be sweet, now, and don't plague me with it, there's plenty of time for you to have babies.

I'm twenty-eight, Blair. My sister is twenty-nine and she has three boys.

Your sister is a brood mare with no commitment, no devotion to the arts.

My sister has a degree in biology and practices the art of teaching. What is my art, Blair? What is my art?

Tell you what, luv, we'll talk about this when I come back. The very moment I step off the plane, we'll have a good long talk about it.

I could go with you . . .

No. *No.* Not that again. You know how I work. You know my actors must feel they have my undivided attention, that I'm utterly devoted to them.

Your actors? Is that the proper gender, Blair?

They discussed it when he came back from Spain. They discussed it when he came back from Italy, from Montana, from Japan, from England. The discussions—like the union—bore no fruit. It was an impasse. Each time Susannah reached the difficult and painful decision to leave him, Blair would leave her to do another picture, and in the reconciliation of parting she was seduced by the vague hope that time and distance would make the difference, would bring her that most cherished of all solutions, her own way.

In the end, it was vanity that caused her to abide by resolutions rent and ragtag from making and unmaking. She left the smooth-faced plains of her twenties and moved reluctantly into the more difficult terrain of moisturizers, diet and exercise. There was the shock of a web of lines around her eyes and whatever is this? A gray hair? How could that be? Only yesterday she had joined that proud sisterhood of the menarche and watched with delight as the pudgy soft flesh around her middle moved down into molded hips and up into high, firm breasts. Now the treacherous chemistry was reversing itself. The breasts were not quite so high, so firm. The waistline began to thicken, and the upper thigh developed a peculiar bulge, unexplainable except in its universality. The tone of the skin began its long irreversible journey. Why did it have to start so early? Why did the body have to spend so many years preparing the soul to be old? Barren thou wert and to barrenness thou returneth.

It was not altogether Blair's affairs with other women; rather, the knowledge that those women were younger.

She packed her things, a small accumulation considering their years together. No china or crystal, painstakingly collected, no heirloom silver to be wrapped in flannel, not even a soup pot or a time-seasoned skillet. The furnished penthouse had furnished everything. No pieces of nostalgia from foreign lands. Blair had brought perfume, hastily picked up in the duty-free shops of the world's airports. No paintings to be divided. Blair had chosen them all, and how like his own art they were—statements on the confusion, the frustration, the small attainments and, worse, the small yearnings of man. No living thing, no dog or cat, to decide custody of. Nothing jointly owned . . . jointly loved.

"Blair said that I was not a loving woman. He said that I was, well, inhibited, cold, and that was why he—"

Pepper's dark eyes glinted in anger. "Don't you believe that, Missy, don't you believe that for one minute! That's jest the excuse they uses when the rut comes on 'em." She looked furtively around the room, then leaned over and whispered in Susannah's ear. "If you git yourself another one that's inclined to stray off, you let me know and I'll send you a recipe." She drew back, sniffed, then pulled out the ruby pin and began to reposition her hat.

"Recipe?" Susannah said, smiling. "Old bayou love potion?"

"No."

"What is it?"

"Special recipe. It gits rid of the problem."

"The . . . ah, the rut?"

Pepper stared at her unblinking, her eyes still full of

anger. "The no-good man. He goes to bed after supper not feelin' so good an' he don't wake up come mornin'."

Susannah watched in openmouthed astonishment as Pepper continued to fuss with the hat and mumble to herself. Pepper, God's handmaiden, offering up deadly recipes for wandering husbands. Good and evil—a two-headed baby that did battle one time and held hands the next.

The kitchen door pushed open and Jason came in, first stomping snow from his feet onto the mat, then wiping them again on the gunnysack inside. "The limousine's coming up the road," he said.

"Is somebody comin' in from the bunkhouse to mind Meg?"

"Lester's here. He went in the front way."

"Did you tell him Meggy was not to go outdoors? She got a little head cold comin' on."

"I told him. Now will you get your coat on. Let's not keep the man waiting."

"Poor Lizbeth ain't in no hurry. You know how Lester is if you don't speak plain with him. He'll jest turn on that television and forgit all about that youngun."

Jason smiled patiently. "Okay, why don't you go speak plain with him, huh, and see if you can round up everybody?"

His eyes followed her out of the kitchen, then he glanced over to where Susannah sat, her hands clenched in her lap, her eyes staring vacantly, straight ahead.

"Good morning, Susannah. Are you all right? You don't look too good."

She sighed and lifted her eyes to his. "I'm all right, Jason. I was just thinking that life is full of surprises."

He nodded sympathetically. "We missed you at supper last night."

"I was tired." She realized he was smiling in his old conciliatory way. The years and the hot dry summers had added lines to his face, but it seemed to her he had changed very little. He had all his hair, still thick and wheat-colored, and now, as he ran his hand through it, it fell over his forehead as it had when he was a young man. The eyes;

they were still the shade of morning glories. Susannah shivered.

Jason extended his hand and, after hesitating for a moment, let it come to rest lightly on her shoulder. "I hope," he said, "we'll have a chance to talk."

She glanced from his face to his hand where it lay on her shoulder, burning through the heavy fabric to bare flesh that still remembered. She smiled and lifted her chin. "We will, Jason, we will."

One by one they drifted into the front hall. Lester was talking about what might be on television, and Pepper was talking about Meg's head cold. Page had his hands in his pockets and wore his usual look of impatience. Meg was wailing loudly that she was so old enough to go to a funeral, and Hodge was telling her it was just like a church service and she knew darn well that wasn't any fun. Kate was pale, detached, standing apart with Marty, waiting.

"Are they going to put Gramma in the ground?" Meg wanted to know. Hodge nodded slowly, as if he had not thought of that possibility. "In a box like when Angel got run over?"

"Yes, but it's called a casket when it's people."

Page shifted from one foot to the other. "Dad," he said loudly, "we're going to be late."

"You're interrupting your brother," Jason answered evenly, and Page folded his arms and turned away.

"It's awful cold, Hodge," Meg said, with mounting concern. "Is she going to Heaven right away?"

"Yes, Meggy. Right away."

"But how'll she get up to the sky if she's in the ground in a box? Does Jesus come down and open the box?"

Hodge licked his lips and glanced at his father.

"You're doing just fine," Jason said.

"You remember when we talked about Angel's soul?" Hodge continued hesitantly.

"Yes. Daddy said we would always remember Angel and what a good dog she was and she would live in our hearts.

But how will Gramma get to Heaven if she's in the ground?"

Hodge looked helplessly at Jason, and Meg started to cry. Jason picked her up and gently wiped her face with his handkerchief. "Meg, we know that nothing really dies, because everything becomes a part of something else. And someone's soul—well, that's so special and so mysterious nobody even knows where it is. So how it gets from one place to another is something we just have to let God take care of. See?"

Meg nodded thoughtfully, twisting her silken hair around her finger, then, mollified, wiggled out of her father's arms and went to stand beside Lester.

"You tell Gramma 'bye for me, Hodge. I better not come 'cause I got a little head cold comin' on."

TEN

THE AIR in the Community House was heavy with the sweet scent of hothouse flowers. The music from the out-of-tune upright was somber and only vaguely familiar. The instrument was much better suited to the boisterous strains of the gospel songs that would come later when the turn-collared man of an alien faith had said his piece and gone his way.

The square frame building had many purposes, and it served them all. With its chairs folded and stacked neatly behind the stage, its walls lined with food-filled tables and a punch mildly laced with white lightning by some adventurous adolescent, its floors echoing the sounds of young whirling feet, older shuffling and still older tapping, it celebrated.

In order and pride, it lined up its healthy young men in front of tables piled high with forms, papers and index cards, judged as many as possible 1-A and dutifully sent them off in airplanes and ships to defend and protect Robina County.

With its chairs again unfolded and in place, it watched radiant girl-women, keeping step with both the music and their fathers, join trembling young men at the end of the aisle from whom only death was meant to part them.

It graduated children with slick hair and ears red with washing. It listened attentively to politicians, faith healers and veterinarians. It welcomed speakers on horticulture, on sanitation, on great books, and (once) sex education, and then counted itself not only well-informed but broad-minded as well.

And, as it did now, it decked itself with flowers, gathered its citizens and its ghosts, and paid its last respects to that which was held most dear: a life, however lived, sacred and awesome in the loss of it.

Susannah felt the differences profoundly. In her adopted city—the land of mink and money, of blondes and blow-jobs, of freeways and freebies—living was carried on with deadly urgency. The object to get. Get the contract, the cash up front, the invitation, the part, the write-off, the broad with the big tits. Dying was for losers, the result of an inadequacy, an unworthiness, a disgraceful inability to cope with the pressures.

Lennie had a coronary on the tennis court. He lost his ass on the last picture. Lost the house, the boat, the Ferrari. Ethel kept the Rolls. Drove it to his grave. Better go to the gym tomorrow. Better have a cholesterol run.

Jesus, not Milly! She was only thirty-eight—well maybe forty, forty-two? You know she took the pills. Oh God yes! Pills to get up with, pills to lose weight, pills to gain weight, pills to sleep, pills to screw, pills to make her fingernails grow. Probably had a few drinks and forgot she'd already taken a handful. Really makes you think, doesn't it, when it's somebody you know, somebody you had lunch with last week, somebody close to your own *age*, for chrissake!

He croaked! The dipshit died! Five years and all that money down the tubes! Thank God it's deductible! Now I have to start all over again with another analyst. Just when things were beginning to happen. Just when I was begin-ning to establish meaningful relationships.

They had this luncheon for her. How 'bout that? She had maybe two weeks left, and they had this gigantic do to raise money, would you believe, in her name for the City of Hope. Let me tell you, it was weird. There she was, the eighty-two-pound guest of honor, acting like some kind of saint or something. I mean you know it's em*bar*rassing. What can you say to somebody like that? Can you believe it? Weird! I tell you, this kind of thing wouldn't happen back East. People out here are so tacky. Of course I went. I wouldn't have missed it for the world.

The piano whined and whinnied on, with Mrs. Wright keeping a heavy foot on the pedal in an effort to bring an organlike quality to bear. The family occupied the first row in full view of the other mourners. To conceal their tears— if there were any—in an alcove behind a thin drape was unnecessary and architecturally unprovided for. Grief was expected, as was a proper amount of restraint.

Father Flesher walked with slow, measured steps to the altar. He nodded to Mrs. Wright, who smiled gratefully and brought the tuneless invocation to a hasty conclusion. Then, to the discomfort of the congregation, he spoke briefly in Latin and crossed himself in the name of the Trinity. He followed this with the tortured pleas of King David's Fifty-first Psalm, and the people relaxed, even silently rejoiced to hear the words "transgressions," "salvation" and "righteousness" replace the foreign and therefore suspect tongue.

"'Have mercy upon me, O God, according to thy lovingkindness; according unto the multitude of thy tender mercies blot out my transgressions. Wash me thoroughly from mine iniquity, and cleanse me from my sin. For I acknowledge my transgressions; And my sin is ever before me. . .'"

What were your sins, Momma? Susannah thought. Your terrible, terrible sins? Sinful to lose your love and not recover? Such a bad, bad sin. Oh, Momma! I think the world sinned against you, and you got no lovingkindness or tender mercies from God or anybody else.

"'. . . .For thou desirest not sacrifice; else would I give it; Thou delightest not in burnt offering. The sacrifices of God are a broken spirit; a broken and contrite heart, O God, thou wilt not despise. . ."

O gracious and loving and egotistical God, if this is what you treasure, a broken heart and a broken spirit, then surely Momma will sit at your right hand and dwell in the house of the Lord forever . . . and ever . . . and ever . . .

As services went, in Robina, this one was brief and (it seemed to the congregation) principally an admonishment to the living to mend their ways. Not that they weren't used to that, but not from a stranger. No, thank you! Besides, they missed the warm and familiar recounting of the deceased's good deeds, shining qualities and lengthy genealogy. There were good things to say about Elizabeth! She had two fine daughters, didn't she! Oh, maybe Susannah's a shade fast, but she'll come around. One of our own should have preached the sermon. This priest didn't even know her. She was a fine God-fearing woman before that horse stomped Adam and she took to drink.

It just wasn't right to put a body away without saying something good over it.

The interment too was brief. In the dark coldness of the canvas tent, Susannah stared dry-eyed at the grasslike blanket that lined the grave, felt sickened by the sweet smell of carnations so soon to die in the snow. As if at a distance, she heard the muffled tears of Hodge, the melodic sobs of Pepper, then suddenly, while Father Flesher spoke of the resurrection and the life, she felt the sharp cold air in her nose, followed it to her lungs, then watched in wonder as it returned in a cloud of frost. She wiggled her stiff toes and was at once aware of blood flowing obediently into them. She counted her heartbeats, felt an exquisite vitality and imagined herself running, arms outstretched, through an open field. She felt the core of herself and sensed the rhythm of its tireless preparations for immortality. And then, filled with shame, she wept for the absence of grief.

Father Flesher returned to Martinsville. The congregation returned to the Community House in Robina. Early in the memorial service the pall was lifted by the combined forces of zest and faith. The walls shook with the gusto of "Shall We Gather at the River," exhilarated in "Shall the Circle Be Unbroken," paused for a recitation of the hymns to death of both Walt Whitman and Edgar A. Guest, then listened as Robinians went backward in time to recapture the Elizabeth Warwick of better, happier days.

One remembered when she first moved to town, a pretty little thing, someplace in the middle of Liam Sullivan's eight children, and how she stayed behind, supported herself working at the A-1 Café when Sullivan gave up on sharecropping and moved his brood to California to pick oranges. Yes, sir! Worked that counter, made her grades, and in her senior year was the highest-scoring forward in the state. Another recalled her wedding day—the Community House had never seen a more beautiful bride, a handsomer couple. A long list of virtues included her scrupulous housekeeping (you could eat off her floor), how well she sat a horse (helped Adam and Gideon with the cattle when she wasn't in a family way), her clear, rich contralto (you wouldn't think a Catholic could belt it out like that, brought up as they were on foreign music), how pretty and clean she kept the babies—until Adam died, of course, and then, well, you never knew when the devil would get a stranglehold on a person, and they prayed that the Lord would take into consideration that better, happier Elizabeth of those better, happier years.

The service closed with a rafter-ringing rendition of "God Will Take Care of You," and the mourners made their way to the Garrity Ranch, where warm fires, hot food, and an endless supply of Pepper's elderberry wine awaited them.

Marty was admiring the generous backside of Marylouise Wright and had just decided to move around to the front of her when he saw Hodge, his face pinched and pale, slip through the crowd and out the back door. He glanced again at Marylouise, sighed, put his full plate on the sideboard and hurried upstairs for his borrowed boots and jacket.

He went directly to the stables and, finding The Sullivan in the paddock, then searched the barn, and after that the cellar, where he found Hodge, huddled forlornly on one of the feather pads, his knees drawn up to his chest, his head resting on his arms.

"Okay if I join you?" Marty said. Hodge nodded, his face still hidden by his arms. "I guess you thought a lot of your grandmother," Marty began after a short silence.

Hodge nodded again. When he spoke, his voice was muffled and scornful. "Most of those people didn't like her, though, they were just putting on an act. Page always called her the dippy drunk, and Mrs. Wright said she was a scarlet woman."

"Do you know what a scarlet woman is?"

Hodge shot him a look of impatience. "Of course I do, Marty. It's a woman who has sex with a man she isn't married to." He shifted uncomfortably. "But that doesn't make somebody bad. Anyhow, she was always good to me."

"That's what really matters, isn't it? How you felt about her."

Hodge sniffed and wiped his nose on the back of his hand. At the memorial service when the people were talking about his grandmother—not *really* his grandmother, he could see that, but some young woman they could recall without embarrassment—his mother had bent across Jason to ask if there was anything Hodge wished to say. He had moved his head quickly from side to side and moved closer to Jason. Now he looked up at Marty, whose face was full of kindness and invitation. Yes, there was so much he wanted to say, to clear up, to give evidence for, to bear witness. It was as if he had been entrusted with his grandmother's real self but, for all his willingness, was unable to discharge such a grave responsibility.

Marty nodded almost imperceptibly, and his eyebrows

arched in interest. "I'd like to hear about your grand-mother," he said quietly.

Both of them were absolutely still for several minutes, then Hodge began to talk in an easy, relaxed way.

"She always had time," Hodge said. "Always. You know, Marty, most grownups don't have much time, time that isn't spoken for. Like Pepper can't make cookies on Tuesday 'cause Friday is cookie day and she has other things for Tuesday. You know what I mean?"

Marty smiled a little wistfully, clearly indicating that he knew about the problems of time.

"And Mom," Hodge went on. "She doesn't have time for anything that isn't schoolwork—you know, important stuff—'cause she's always busy correcting papers or doing something for the church or the PTA or. . ." His voice trailed off and he looked distracted for a moment as his eyes followed the rows of clean glass Mason jars that lined the shelves in front of him. "Jason's pretty good," he continued, "but running this kind of ranch is a full-time job and he doesn't have time for—well, you know, just time."

He grinned and his face brightened. "But Gramma! Now, Gramma had time. She'd make cookies any old day, just because it was a good day for it. All of a sudden she'd say, 'How 'bout some peanut-butter cookies fresh out of the oven,' and she'd drop whatever she was doing and go make a batch.

"And when you'd tell her about something, any little old thing, she always paid attention. She'd look right at you and listen to what you were saying. And if the phone rang or something like that, she'd say, 'Go on with your story, Hodgie, they'll call back if it's important.'"

He sniffed again, then took the handkerchief Marty offered and blew his nose. He sighed and fell into a long silence, and Marty leaned back, stretched his legs out in front of him, hoping to look like a someone with all the time in the world.

"The thing is," Hodge said finally, "that they always say they'd really like to do that if they just had the time but they can't 'cause they've got all these other things to do that they don't really want to do." He shook his head in be-wilderment. "It just doesn't make sense to me." And then he smiled again, the wide smile of a pleasant memory. "You know those silly things little kids make in school? You know, pictures out of macaroni shells and stuff like that?" Marty nodded agreeably, even though this sort of thing was not part of his experience. "Well," Hodge went on, "every dumb thing that Patrick and Meg brought home, she'd make a big fuss over and put up with thumbtacks in the living room. Mom always moved 'em to the kitchen, but Gramma just put up the next bunch like she didn't even notice."

He stopped abruptly, shook his head back and forth slowly and hunched himself forward like someone having a chill. Marty could hardly hear his words when he spoke. "I think that scarlet-woman stuff is bullshit. What do you suppose it really was? Why do you suppose some folks wouldn't speak to her when she passed them on the street?"

"I don't know, Hodge. Maybe they were just afraid."

"Of Gramma?"

"Well, I think there's some of your Gramma in all of us, a part of ourselves that wants to be free, not to have any responsibilities, to go make a batch of cookies whenever we feel like it, to pack up and leave the scene whenever we get bored or fed up. But most of us just can't do that. We've got to run the ranch or correct the papers, pay the bills, keep up the good work. You know what I mean?"

"Yes, sir."

"Well, along comes your grandmother breezing into town from whereever she's been and it must seem to these hardworking folks like she's laughing at them. You know: Hey, you dolts! You've taken a wrong turn! Life is out there, dancing on the mountains and singing in the streets. It's all you've got. Is this what you really meant to do with it? So, the part of them that was bored and fed up got mad at her for reminding them that there was another world out there."

Hodge was thoughtful, wrinkling heavy lines across his forehead and tapping his foot against a bean barrel. "Well," he said finally, "that's probably what I'll do, go out there in that other world."

"Oh? What'll you do out there?"

"Ummm, I might rodeo for a while, knock around the country, get a job on a freighter going to Alaska. I'd take my time about settling down. With my experience I could get on with a big ranch out West cowboyin', maybe later even save some money and get my own spread."

"What's wrong with this ranch? Seems to me you've got a good deal here."

"No."

"Why not? I mean, after you've knocked around the country for a while?"

"No," Hodge repeated firmly. "I don't belong here."

"How come? Looks to me like you're your dad's right-hand man."

Hodge smiled wanly, and a heavy solemness settled over him. "I haven't told anybody," he said wearily. "I didn't even talk to Gramma about it." He was quiet for a moment, pulling his lower lip into his mouth, biting into it with his small, even teeth, tapping with his foot more sharply on the barrel. Then suddenly, in a rush, he blurted out the words, "Jason's not my real dad."

Marty was puzzled. "You mean you're adopted?"

"No," Hodge answered simply.

Marty stared at him, then took a deep breath. "Do you know that for sure, Hodge? You know, a lot of kids have these fantasies about their parents."

Hodge stopped him with a direct, unblinking gaze. "For sure," he said quietly.

"How do you know?"

"Page. He told me, said I should know the truth."

"Your brother," Marty said dryly, "seems to have some direct line to what's best for everybody."

"It doesn't matter. I knew before he told me. There are things that you just *know*."

"Have you spoken to your folks about this?" Marty asked, knowing the answer, stalling for time and inspiration.

"Oh no!" Hodge said quickly. "I'll never tell them. It would really hurt Jason, and God knows what Mom would do." His eyes narrowed into menacing slits and he squared his shoulders. "I told Page I'd have his hide if he took a notion to say anything to them. I don't want them to know I know about it. I just want to disappear someday and make my own way in the world."

"But don't you think that would hurt them more? If you just left without a word?"

"They'd get over it. They've got Page and Meg and Pat that they planned on. I wasn't even planned on, I was an accident that happened to Mom." Marty moved to accommodate an uncomfortable knotting in his gut. "It's hard enough," Hodge went on, "to imagine Mom doing—well, you know—*that*. I guess I sound like a little kid. I mean I know all about sex and all that, but it's still hard even to think of her and Jason, let alone. . ."

His voice cracked, and Marty moved closer and put his arm around his shoulders. He felt a sudden unease and impatience with the rest of the world. It was as if the two of them were accomplices, and he wanted to give Hodge something—something so the boy could, with honor, allow the man to carry part of this awesome burden. Painfully aware of the meagerness of his gift, he held out the bond of an injury of his own. "You know," he said softly, "when I was about your age—a little younger, I guess—Charlie Kleinfelter told me all about it, about what people did to make babies. Oh, I knew where they came from, but I hadn't given any deep thought to how they got there. Charlie's description didn't have any love in it, not even any good healthy lust. Strictly porno. Besides that, but I didn't know it then, it wasn't even accurate. Well, I wiped up the street with that asshole, and while I was beating on him I was yelling at him, over and over, 'Maybe my dad, but not my *mother!*'" He paused and hugged Hodge closer to him. "And then," he sighed, "I sat down on the curb and cried."

Sobbing and choking, Hodge buried his face against the chest of a man he had known for only three short days and who held him without reticence or pretense, while for the last time he wept the free-flowing tears of childhood.

ELEVEN

THE SKY cast off the somber gray drape it had worn the previous day for Elizabeth's funeral, revealing a bright, gaudy blue beneath. The midmorning sun shone in a dazzling false spring on the snow and melted it into rivulets and streams and muddy puddles just right for the sailing of small boats, the building of levees and locks, the making of oozing brown delicacies, and—as if by accident—for splashing in. Meg and Patrick, their instincts not yet seriously hampered by ongoing civilizing processes, and with an enthusiasm that chagrined their mother, who would have preferred less outright cheerfulness, answered the call of sky, sun and mudhole.

"They forget so quickly," Kate observed as she watched them from the sunroom window.

Susannah put a marker in the book she was reading and placed it on the table beside her. "I don't think they've forgotten," she said, smiling affectionately, "not really. They just handle it in a different way. After all, they don't feel guilty like we do."

"Guilty?"

"Sure. I suspect if we had loved her more, we'd be able to mourn her less."

Kate turned and leaned against the sewing machine. "I don't think I understand what you mean." Her voice had a sharp edge to it, and she felt the same vague irritation and apprehension that always followed her sister's self-assured pronouncements, ready assessments, and easy solutions. Unaccountably, she saw herself kneeling at the coffee table in front of the fire, lavishing her full twelve-year-old attention on the thousand-piece puzzle, searching patiently for the one piece (it would have a brighter green on one arm) that would connect this part with this part and produce one finished corner. Here comes Susannah, breezing through, pausing to hover, pursing her lips, and deftly plucking a piece from the pile, fitting it in with a flourish. Smiling. Expecting gratitude.

But Susannah was not speaking with the assurance of someone who held the missing piece. She said, "Earlier Meg told me she was going to make Gramma's favorite mud tart, and she went on about how Momma used to help decorate them. It was such a warm, pleasant memory for her. What memories do we have? Mostly of a phantom coming and going."

"She was our mother," Kate objected.

"She gave birth to us, yes, and she hung around for a couple of years, and she dropped in now and then. Don't get all stiff like that, Kate. We won't be struck by lightning. I'm not speaking ill of the dead, I'm just trying to figure things out."

Kate shook her head. "I don't see how you can compare our feelings to those of the children."

"But we were children once. We don't completely outgrow it like shoes and dresses. The girl you is a part of the woman you. Don't you see? I *think*," Susannah went on thoughtfully, drawing out her words, "that those two little girls probably wondered what on earth they'd done that was so awful, so god-awful, it would make their mother leave them. You've got to be pretty dreadful if your own momma can't stomach you."

"Oh, children don't think like that."

"Maybe not consciously, but it's there all the same. Patrick and Meg have good memories, good thoughts about Momma, and that's why they're out there laughing and playing—not because of what they've forgotten, but because of what they remember. See? And here we are in sackcloth and ashes, still trying to figure out where we went wrong."

Kate turned away. The problem was she didn't know *how* to respond to this uncommon earnestness, this hesitant offer of the intimacy of a shared failure. They had been such devoted enemies for such a very long time, it was unnerving to think that some other kind of relationship had ever been, could ever be, possible. Still, one had to start somewhere. She smiled. "I'm so glad you've decided to stay for a while. Maybe we'll get to know each other a little better."

The hush that followed was broken by a polite tap on the door; then Marty's head appeared. "Excuse me, ladies, I'm after my gear." Both of them stared at him with blank, distracted faces. "Hello—hello there," he said loudly. "It's me. Martin Stone from Los Angeles. Anybody home?"

Susannah laughed and jumped up from her chair. "I'm sorry, love, we're in shock. Kate and I have broken a record—we've been in the same room for thirty minutes and haven't declared war." She glanced at her watch. "Is it time? For you to go, I mean?"

"The plane leaves at two, we should get started soon."

Susannah looked around the room. "You all ready?"

"Just about. Hodge is getting some pickles for the basket of goodies Pepper's putting together." He turned and put both hands on Kate's shoulders. "I really mean what I said. Send him out this summer and I'll teach him to play polo."

Kate laughed. "Really, Marty, what would a busy man like you do with an eleven-year-old?"

He was still holding her shoulders, and bent down to kiss her cheek. "I'd keep him, that's what I'd do—never send him home." He moved across the room and collected his bags from the brass bed.

It came to Kate that this was not an idle invitation, that there existed between her son and this man a very special affection, and she realized that she felt grateful for it.

Later, on the drive to the airport, Marty roused himself suddenly out of a contemplative silence and thumped his knee with his palm. "Yes, sir," he said. "Yes, indeed! That's really a first-rate group back there." Susannah smiled and nodded in agreement. "I take it," Marty went on, looking pleased, "that you and Kate are patching things up?"

"We're working on it."

"And Jason?"

Susannah flushed, and said coolly, "That's no problem, there's nothing there to patch."

"Ummmm." Marty worked the dials on the radio, finally brought in a station without static—the country-and-western station in Martinsville—and they rode without speaking, Susannah tapping her foot, for several miles. As they crossed the railroad tracks outside Robina, Marty turned to her and asked, "How long you think you'll stay?"

"Don't know for sure. Maybe till I finish the *Cosmo* article—a week? I don't go back on the chicken-and-peas circuit till May. Unless I get a new date on the Baltimore thing."

"What's the *Cosmo* piece?"

"Don't know, they haven't told me yet."

Marty sighed and shifted in his seat. "Don't you get tired of that?"

"Tired of what, love?"

"Muck," he said shortly. "What was the last thing you did for them? Something about creative infidelity?"

She shrugged. "It's a living." Then turned to look at him, puzzled. "What the hell's the matter with you?"

Marty looked equally puzzled. "I don't know, honey. I'm sorry, never mind, forget it."

"Forget what? What is it?"

He pulled off one glove with his teeth and reached into his shirt pocket for his cigarettes, took one, put the pack on the dashboard and pushed in the lighter with his thumb. Susannah watched and waited. Marty smoked with a drink, with coffee, or when he had a criticism to deliver. "Well," he said finally, "I guess it's that I've seen you in a different light here. Kind of reminds me of the old days when you wanted to do something important." Susannah hummed mournfully and drew an imaginary bow across her out-stretched arm. "Okayokay," he said, "so it *is* cornball, but where's the lady who said she worked in the world?"

"Honest to God, Marty! I don't know what's got into you."

"Okay, for instance, the month we lost Hammarskjöld, your big schtick was a bullfighter who got it in the crotch and a phony discourse on the death of gallantry."

She laughed and poked him in the ribs. "If it was good enough for Hemingway—"

"And after the President was shot," he persisted, "you did a piece of trash on the sort of man who would win Jackie's hand." He looked pained. "Shall I go on?" She lit a cigarette and turned her head to look out the window. "I go on. It's not like you were some asshole redneck who doesn't know if Cambodia's a Mexican beer or a hooker in Détroit. You know what's going on and you used to get involved in it. Now you just stick your head up there in the clouds, say ta-ta and skip merrily through five thousand yards of shit."

"Marty, either shut up or stop the car and I'll get out and walk. I don't need this."

He took one hand off the wheel and turned it palm up-ward. "All I'm trying to say is you might at least look down once in a while. You might at least look down and say, Jeez, how 'bout that, my feet are dirty." She glared at him and reached for the door handle. "Okay," he said quickly, "okay, no more."

They rode in a chilled silence until he drove the car into the passenger loading zone at the airport. He turned off the ignition and turned to face her, his arm resting on the seat behind her.

Susannah looked at her watch. "You'll miss your plane," she said crisply.

"There's still time. And there's time for you, too. Come on in, the water's fine."

She raised one brow and looked at him from the corner of her eye. "And then what?"

"Maybe you'll find that when you're up to your neck doing something you do well, you won't have to be doing yourself in so often."

"Doing myself in," she said, in a voice that contrived to be arch and questioning at the same time.

"Doing work you're ashamed of, marrying the wrong men." He paused, considering the offense that was uppermost in his mind, the one that, until two days before, he had not allowed to trouble him.

"Are you finished?" she said, peering at him closely.

Marty cleared his throat and looked away from her. "And," he said, very quietly, "wearing the Marlboro Man around your neck like an old sack of garlic."

Her expression didn't change. She took her purse from the seat beside her, unzipped it and rummaged around inside. "Do I give you a check now, Doctor, or do you send me a bill?" she asked pleasantly.

He sighed and glanced at his watch. "You're right, gotta go." He leaned over and kissed her lightly on her thin, frozen smile. "Don't be mad at me, okay?" He got out of the car, went around to the trunk, took his bags and set them on the curb.

Susannah slid across to the driver's seat and rolled down the window. Slowly, she brought her finger up and aimed it at his heart. "Perhaps," she said, in a low, dangerous voice, "we should do *your* hangups." And as she framed them in her mind, readied them for speech, she suddenly recognized the power in the words she could either speak or withhold, as she chose. She could parade them out like a firing squad: Caroline; the baby; the year-long drunk; the woman he lived with who tried to kill him with the fireplace tools; unacknowledged faults, hidden vanities, an ammunition dump collected during the undefended moments of a long association.

She stared at him as he stood on the curb, one hand in his trousers pocket, his shoulders slightly hunched against the wind that blew off the airfield, smiling apprehensively, with not the slightest notion of how vulnerable he was at this moment.

She uncocked her finger and reached out to him with her open hand. "Another time, I guess," she said, feeling the anger dissipated by a sweeping, overwhelming sorrow. "I don't have anything that's fair trade at the moment."

He put his head through the window and kissed her again, finding her mouth soft this time. Then he stepped back, waved and walked toward the entrance.

Susannah watched him until he disappeared into the terminal, wondering if that mournful tolling, that hollow lonely knell in her ears could, by any stretch of the imagination, be considered . . . bells?

She stopped off in the kitchen to tell Pepper she would be down to help with dinner after she showered and made a couple of phone calls. Pepper said she didn't need any help but she would welcome the company, adding that Kate had gone off with Marylouise, Jason into Martinsville, and the younguns were scattered only the Lord knew where—with the four winds. All this gallivanting around was not, to her way of thinking, proper behavior in a house of mourning.

Susannah resisted the temptation to set forth her own theory on the subject and mumbled something she hoped sounded like agreement. She poured herself a cup of coffee and climbed the stairs to her room, where she sank gratefully into the rocker by the bed. So tired, so deep-down, bone-marrow weary. All those emotional push-ups, all that energy flailing about, and she hadn't a clue as to how she felt about any of it—her mother, Kate, Marty, not even her work, which had ceased to concern her when it stopped giving her pleasure. At least she thought it had.

As she sat sipping the coffee, considering with tepid interest her own ragged sensibilities, the late-afternoon sun began to juggle rainbows on the cut edges of the perfume bottles on the dressing table. In the center of the table there was a thick black book, and on top of it a bundle of papers. She gazed at them for several minutes before her curiosity got the better of her lethargy and moved her body across the room. The black book was a photograph album filled with old sepia prints, many of them of that young girl, that young woman, whom the people of the town had remembered at yesterday's service. There was a note from Kate that said she had found the album among their mother's things and thought Susannah might enjoy looking at it. Enjoy? Oh, Kate! The bundle was a thick packet of letters, ivory-colored with age and tied with a black shoestring. There was no note. She untied the string and flipped through the envelopes, recognizing on each her own hurried, rounded hand. They were, it appeared, in chronological order. Tidy Kate's work, no doubt, she thought as she opened the one on top.

DEAR GRAN & PEPPER

Well I got here! I'm staying with Marylouise's cousin JoAnne in a fabulous apartment in Westwood. My bedroom has a balcony that looks out over a huge courtyard and a swimming pool and there are movie stars every place.

The trip was wonderful—the scenery was BEAU-TIFUL and the best thing was eating in the dining car while it all moved by. (There were white tablecloths and a rose in a silver vase on each table) AND THE FOOD!!! There's this thing called a Cornish Game Hen. WONDERFUL! I had it while I was looking at New Mexico which is as flat and barren as western Oklahoma but so beautiful and sort of pure. Then there's something called hollandaise sauce and its so good you want to rub it all over you! Had that in Arizona while I was looking at the mesas that just crop up out of nowhere and turn red and blue and purple when the light changes. (The hollandaise sauce is yellow)

The last night on the train I ordered trout and the waiter brought me some lime sherbet right along with it. Well I thought that HE thought that I was some kind of hick so I told him nicely that I'd have my desert later thank you. He kinda laughed and said the sherbet was to clear the palate. Just imagine! I got to be almost twenty years old before I learned that!

Early the next morning the porter came by calling LOS ANGELES. I jumped up and got dressed and went to the observation car. You can't imagine how beautiful it is! So much color and mountains and palm trees and orange groves and pink houses—PINK houses.

I'm going to take this to the post office now and then I'll go get a job and then to the library and see if I can find a recipe book with hollandaise sauce in it.

Don't worry about me. I'm having a wonderful time—not homesick at all.

PLEASE WRITE!!!!

Love,
Missy

"Don't worry about me," Susannah said aloud. "I'm having a wonderful time. . ."

In the vast, resounding catacombs of the Kansas City station, she had felt a mounting panic, a terrible feeling of isolation. She smiled at the redcap, gave him fifty cents and a nervous "Thank you." He looked at his open palm, told her he had to turn in seventy-five cents for three suitcases and pointed to a sign over his head. She reached into her bag, dropped her gloves, bent over to pick them up and spilled the contents of the purse: makeup, change, sunglasses, papers, falling and flying into the pathway of the first unmindful feet she had ever known.

She spent most of her time in the observation car staring out the wide windows into the flat, endless desert. Jason's face was the mirage that rose up in front of the distant mesas, in the sudden, small whirlwinds that rearranged the white sand. She went to the dining car because her strong young body wanted to be fed and sent her there, but thoughts of the picnics at the creek caused her head to lose its appetite, so she picked at the Cornish game hen, drew lines with her fork in the hollandaise sauce.

The porter called "Los Angeles," and the train clicked on and on, past scrubby backyards, square boxes of houses huddled together, connected by an endless stretch of flapping clothesline. The mirage was there, too, in the white upside-down shirts. So that when she got off the train, half a continent away from Robina, she carried Jason with her, packed in her going-away baggage.

Well, there's not a whole hell of a lot of room, said JoAnne, but you sure are welcome if you don't mind being cramped.

And they borrowed a folding bed from the landlord and put it into the breakfast room, then cleaned out the broom closet for Susannah's clothes. There was a balcony. It overlooked the Mormon Temple.

DEAR GRAN & PEPPER,
Well! It's easier to find a recipe than it is to find a JOB! I'm enrolled in a typing course. (The lady at the employment agency said I had no marketable skills.)

JoAnne arranged an interview for me with a friend of hers who owns a kind of talent agency. He thinks I show a lot of promise and all I need is a little experience—exposure they call it out here. His name is Marty Stone and he looks like a combination of Tony Curtis and Gregory Peck and a hot fudge sundae when you need to gain weight! Tomorrow I have an appointment about a part time job with an advertising agency. It's small—what's called a "one man shop" and the one man's ONE account is a thing called NIFTY SWIFTY THE MIRACLE PEELER. With this great boon to mankind, he peels carrots and potatoes and the like right there on television. If I get the job Pepper I'll send you one. And thank you for sending my clothes and for sending them

with the buttons and hooks and eyes all on. And thank
you Gran for the money.

Please PLEASE write. I miss and love you both.

Always,
MISSY

He said, kindly but firmly, that the Hollywood Hills
were overgrown with such as Susannah, that in fact there
had been an assorted dozen of her—Homecoming Queen
types—through his office just that day. He added that unless she had some outstanding talent or driving ambition
she should forget the whole thing and go back to school.

But if you decide to stick it out and get a couple of jobs on
your own to prove you're serious about this, then I'll consider taking you on—as a favor to Jo.

DEAR GRAN & PEPPER

Oh Pepper! The pickles are MARVELOUS! Jo
says to thank you too. Good news! I got the Nifty-
Swifty job and I'm a sort of jack-of-all-trades here. I
type a little. I answer the phone. I make coffee. I
interview girls looking for commercials to do AND—
pay close attention now—next saturday night I get my
big chance. Mr. Green has been giving me lessons in
how to do a pitch—that's what the Nifty-Swifty commercial is, a pitch. Believe me, it isn't easy to talk fast
and peel all those vegetables at the same time, especially since the Nifty-Swifty just isn't all it's cracked
up to be.

Anyhoo, my typing is up to forty words a minute so
if I flunk vegetable peeling I can always get a real job
with my marketable skill. I don't know exactly where
I'm going, but I'm making progress.

Yes Gran I do remember that Kate graduates in
February. I won't forget to send something. And no, it
does not bother me one whit that she and Jason are
keeping company. There's no question in my mind but
what they deserve each other.

I do wish I could make it home for Christmas but I just can't take the time from my career. But I'll be thinking of you.

Love,
Susannah SULLIVAN

P.S. That's my new stage name—tell Momma if she happens to drop in over the holidays.

She was not bothered by the carefully worded message from Gran that Kate and Jason were keeping company, because she knew it could not possibly be true, that in a week or so she would hear the mail slide through the slot and there would be a letter from him, asking her to come home, begging forgiveness. Or that one day soon she would open the door and he'd be there on a white horse, that he would scoop her up into his arms and carry her into the future. It was only a matter of time.

SEASON'S GREETINGS!
Jo and I had a tree and it looked like a real Christmas with all the wonderful things you all sent underneath it. Thank you for the nice blouse, Kate—I'll wear it with the black velvet skirt (Thank you Gran and thanks for the check) What a gorgeous cosmetic case, Momma, just perfect for my Nifty-Swifty travels and the stuffed whale is enchanting. PEPPER! What a scrumptious assortment of goodies! I made popovers Christmas morning and we had the boysenberry jam with them. THANK YOU! ONE AND ALL!
Mr. Stone is a man of his word. He sent me on a cattle call (that's Hollywood for an interview where everybody in town shows up and the faint hearted get trampled underfoot) for Hotchkins, Whalen and Wheeler. Mr. Whalen used to be in musical comedy on Broadway and he has this idea for a commercial where NOT ONE, NOT TWO, BUT ONE DOZEN lovely ladies and one large sheep dog emerge joyfully and (duck Gran) in near nakedness (not the dog) swing-

ing their hips in time to the music from a fifteen-piece orchestra, from the plush innards of the new Plymouth Stationwagon. I still can't believe I got the job! The girls out here are so breathtaking you can't believe it and every last one of them has these enormous you-know-whats—ENORRR-MUS!

Anyway I showed up last Tuesday with my new bathing suit and my platform shoes. They gave all of us these mink stoles and we trailed them behind us like Zeigfeld girls down a red-carpeted staircase . . .

Susannah smiled and let the letter fall into her lap. So long ago—had she really been that young? It was like reading someone else's mail. Yes, Marty Stone was a man of his word, but he'd been against it from the first.

All those big boobs, she moaned. Nobody'll even see *me*.

You really want somebody to see you in this piece of shit?

Of course I do. This is exposure.

You might call it that— He met her glare with upraised palms. Okayokay, so you want to spend your life in a vacuum. Go out and buy yourself the plainest one-piece suit you can find—knit, you know, honest. No padding, see? And some shoes with really high heels so you won't look like a dwarf. She nodded, and he went on in a kind of monotone. You ask the makeup man to go a little easy. You're the wholesome, whole-milk type. You get there early for makeup, then you go to the studio and make friends with the dog.

With the dog?

With the dog, with the dog, already. Didn't you read the script? The broad who handles the dog has a little extra business. Now, there's the bit where the girls line up on the stairs. You ask the agency producer if it's okay if you stand on the first step because you're nearsighted and you have a little trouble with stairs.

I'm not nearsighted.

I know, but you've got two left feet. Be pleasant, businesslike, easy to get along with, and smile—wholesomely.

No goo-goo eyes at the director. You're there to do a job. They like to lay dumb blondes, but they don't like to work with them. You got all this?

She nodded, looking somewhat dazed, thinking he was right about her feet and wondering if she could possibly remain upright in high-heeled shoes.

Now then—this is important. When you start your walk, look straight into the camera and think about the sun coming up over the Grand Canyon with the New York Philharmonic in the background. Y'know?

Her eyes widened in recognition and a smile spread across her face. Oh yes, I *know*, she said. What are they playing?

What?

What is the New York Philharmonic playing?

I don't know what they're playing, Susannah. Whatever makes you happy.

Mozart? Is that okay? I really like the C Minor Concerto. Jo plays it all the time.

That might be a little too intellectual. How about one of the Russians.

Too sad. I need something to make the sun rise in my heart, not just over the canyon. What do you think?

I can't believe I'm having this conversation, that's what I think. Susannah, you'll have to handle your own music, I'm just the choreographer here. Okay?

Sure, Marty.

Somebody'll see you. I promise.

She was seen, and she spent the next months opening doors—doors to automobiles, doors to refrigerators, doors to washing machines, and doors to the offices of advertising agencies. She was pretty enough to get through the doors, but lacked the glamor that could alienate the large market of female customers who sat in judgment at the other end of the camera. Hers was a face a young mother could identify with; an open, clean-eyed face with no disturbing smolders from inner heat, no sensuous lines of suffering. She was very busy, and she was very disappointed.

She sat with her legs pulled up under her on the couch in Marty's office. Outside, a spastic shower halfheartedly washed the sidewalks and streets. The windows looked out on Sunset Boulevard near Vine, closed to the traffic sounds, the chill and the rain that couldn't make up its mind.

She looked up from the script. God! Five times a week for a month? Can't you get me a talk commercial, Marty?

I told you it was a vacuum.

But if I could at least *talk*. Then maybe I wouldn't feel like such an idiot. I'm a walking, breathing prop.

You can't talk, you've got a twang, you talk through your nose.

I could take lessons. My brain's getting cobwebs in it.

Marty rolled his chair away from the desk and leaned toward her. Honey, he said with a heavy sigh, why don't you go back to school. You're a nice, bright, half-educated girl and you haven't got the instincts for this business. You can't hack it.

I graduated from vegetable-peeling with honors.

He shook his head. You're good for another five, six, maybe seven years and then the lines start to set in. You get big in the can, saggy here, baggy there, and you're washed up, finished, out to pasture.

But I don't *intend* to drag a mink stole behind me forever. Why can't you get me an audition for *Playhouse 90* or something like that?

Marty covered his face with his hands, then ran them through his hair. Because, he said patiently, because, dear heart, you are without a doubt the worst actress I have seen in all my years in the business.

She lit a cigarette and chewed reflectively on her thumbnail. Well, I think I'll take the talking lessons anyway. There's got to be something else I can do. I've had it up to here with the Grand Canyon, and besides, I'm running out of symphonies. So there! She grinned—wholesomely for his benefit—and stood up. Just to show you that my feelings aren't hurt, I'll let you buy me one of Mr. Beefeater's martinis and one of Mr. Cobb's salads.

DEAR KATE:

Under the circumstances, I mean the way things turned out with the farm and with Jason, I can hardly see how you can harp about taking my leavings. What Jason says is probably true. We were fortunate to find out that we didn't really need each other and I suppose that's what marriage is really all about. I read recently that a real bond exists when someone plays a role in the life of another that no other individual can play. It seems obvious that this was not true in our case.

I'm working the month of April, so I won't be able to come for the wedding. But thank you for your kind invitation.

Regards,
SUSANNAH

What's the matter, didn't we pay the electric bill? Sorry I'm late, the script changes didn't come back from mimeo until seven. Are you awake?

Yes.

What's the matter?

I'm thinking about my heavy-booted lover.

Is that Emily or Amy?

My sister is going to marry my heavy-booted lover in April. April, the unkindest month of all.

Oh dear! Sounds like you could use a shoulder. Is this what we're drinking?

It's 'most all gone. There's another bottle in the kitchen.

Jo poured herself a drink, kicked off her shoes and settled down on the pillows in front of the fireplace. You got a letter from Jason?

No. From Sister Kate. She wanted my blessing or maybe just the promise that I wasn't going to swoop down on her happy home. Anyone who knows of any reason why these two . . . There was something about God too. She's always getting God involved in some mess.

Did you expect to go back to him? Did you expect him to come looking for you?

I don't know what I expected, Jo. Certainly not this! It's less than a year. How can you love somebody one minute and marry somebody else the next? It isn't just Jason—I mean it is and it isn't. I can't explain it. There are days when I can't even see his face clearly, can't hear his voice, but there's never a moment that I don't remember what it felt like going to meet him, waiting for him to come. I'm afraid that it won't ever happen again—like that. That I'll go through the rest of my life and never feel it again.

Was he really your—you know, heavy-booted lover?

Yes. But then when Grampa died, he was ashamed. He felt we'd done wrong, and that made me ashamed, too.

Maybe you should go home? Try to work things out?

No. It's too late.

Well then, the thing to do is to get very, very busy. Meet some new people. Work harder, play harder.

Does that do it?

No. But as time goes along you don't notice it so much. The important thing is not to feed it. Take it from someone who's been there. You can make a whole career out of being wretched.

Everything changed. Nothing changed. The weeks became months with no falling snow, no sudden blooming, no orange-gold dying. Susannah opened another refrigerator door. April came quickly and went slowly. Susannah smiled across a breakfast table into the eye of the camera and sipped coffee fit for the gods. And then she woke up one morning and a year had passed.

She opened another door. Wore a pink cloud of tulle at Jo's wedding. Coughed, then dosed herself to immediate recovery. Sent an imported handmade bunting and a one-hundred-dollar bond to Page Gideon Garrity, seven pounds, four ounces. Got hair squeaky clean, clothes whiter-than-white, floors shiny as glass, breath kissing sweet, and herself chock full of energy and goodness. And then one morning she woke up and another year had passed.

For the first time Marty expressed pleasure about sending her on an interview. I think you'll like this kind of thing, he said, and you'll probably do it well. Hosting a morning movie. That's what the world's coming to. The broads are watching old movies at nine o'clock in the morning.

Interviews and stuff like that?

And you'll have a free hand getting guests—you know, a chance to get some really good people.

I still talk through my nose sometimes.

So? Personalities don't have to sound like they come from Nowhere, U.S.A. The producer saw you on that game show and he thinks you sound bright. Here. He handed her a copy of *Newsweek*. Catch up on the world and go have a chat with him. You've got nothing to lose but a little time.

Susannah took the magazine and stared at the cover. She said, But time goes so quickly here, Marty. Marty? Have you noticed that?

DEAR FAMILY,

Hodge is a lovely name—Hodge Morgan Garrity has a lovely ring to it! I suppose aunthood is as close as I'll ever get to motherhood at the rate I'm going. I work all day at the station and am still going to LA City College at night. (The depth and breadth of my ignorance is wondrous to behold!) There's a rumor going around about cutting the movie and just doing the interviews. The ratings have been quite good. And an additional rumor about syndicating the show. I hope it comes to pass because it's likely you'd be able to get it there and there are some things I'd like you to see, things I'm really proud of. I'm beginning to recognize the difference—not just between lousy and pretty good but between pretty good and really something. Homo sapien—sapien, literally "to taste." To *know* what you taste.

I interviewed a man last week who has a theory that aggression has to do with a particular chemical in the brain. He says (and has data to support it) that the level of this chemical continues to drop as we evolve and that eventually aggressive behavior will no longer be adaptive, and the brain will discard the chemical just as the body has discarded the fourth molar. I am much taken with the thought that we may be a stage in our own evolution and that it has nothing at all to do with Good and Evil, but simply with what's adaptive. Is a tiger evil? Of course not. But a burning-bright example of a fierce and hard way of life. *We* had to be fierce too, to get this far, but perhaps one day . . .?

Something important is happening to me here, and if I tend it well, I may grow into something truly useful. Kisses for the babies and love to all.

Late in January the station manager intruded on Susannah's dream of a show of sustained high quality and told her that in sowing the flowers of merit she had let weeds grow up around the ratings. The show was slipping, the audience was yawning, the accounts were canceling. No one, he said, was interested in cultural deprivation—whatever the hell that was—in a preacher who believed that all religious doctrines had historical significance and would she please for chrissake quit reviewing *books!* Nobody was interested in the dangers of insecticides, nobody wanted to hear about water pollution, it was depressing! For chrissake leave off with the scientists, the philosophers, the nursery-school teachers. Controversy! Bizarre people, inflammatory issues, sensationalism—of these ingredients bigger ratings were made. Get some nut to talk about astrology or cosmetic breast surgery. For chrissake, Susannah! For chrissake!

Marty said, Why don't you just go on with what you're doing and see what happens.

I know exactly what'll happen. I'll get fired.

Maybe we can get another station interested.

Do you really think so?

No, not really.

So why beat my head up against a brick wall?

Depends on how important it is to you.

It's important to me to succeed in this business. I can't afford another failure at my age.

Marty smiled but did not comment on Susannah's advanced years. Instead he said, Then what's the problem? Just follow instructions and collect the money when you pass Go.

Susannah leaned over and searched through the letters scattered at her feet. She found what she was looking for and reread the words very slowly. She closed her eyes and tried to recapture the feeling that must have gone into the writing of it; the romantic idealism, the quiet rejoicing, the passionate need to wrap her arms around life . . . *and if I tend it well, I may grow into something truly useful* . . .

"I wrote that," she whispered, trying to remember the moment when terminal cynicism had set in. "I wonder if there's any of that left."

TWELVE

THE NEXT morning, at his office, Marty received a telegram:

> TITLE OF NEW PIECE ROBINA OUR TOWN USA. USUALS MAY NOT WANT IT. YOUR OFFICE MAY HAVE TO PEDDLE IT AND EARN YOUR MONEY FOR A CHANGE.
>
> FONDLY
> YOUR DIRTY FOOTED WORLD WORKER

THIRTEEN

"GOOD MORNING, Pepper."

"Mornin'."

"Good morning, Jason."

"Good morning, Susannah."

"Where is everybody?"

"They all gone off to school. It's near the middle of the day."

Susannah frowned and checked her watch. "It's nine-thirty-five."

"You want breakfast or lunch?"

"Just coffee. I'll get it."

"We got fresh bread just come outa the oven and some nice blackberry preserves."

"Ummmm. Well . . ."

"I had some paperwork to do," Jason said, to no one in particular.

Pepper turned from the breadboard and looked at him disdainfully over her half-glasses. "So?" she said

Jason shifted in his chair. "I was just explaining why I'm still here."

Pepper's look was as sharp as the knife blade she held poised over the loaf of bread. "Um hum."

Susannah yawned. Whatever was rubbing Pepper the wrong way would have to wait until after coffee. She carried the pot to the table. "More for you, Jason?"

"No, guess I'd better get back to work." He stood up, stretched, and asked casually, "What're you going to do today?"

"Oh, I thought maybe I'd take a ride." She laughed and eased herself onto one of the oak chairs. "My butt has just about recovered from the other day." She glanced at Pepper and amended her words. "My backside, that is."

"Take Cindy," Jason said. "She single-foots, smoothest ride on the ranch."

"Is her stuff by her stall?"

"No. Let me know when you're ready and I'll help you."

Susannah nodded and glanced again at Pepper. "If," she laughed, "Pepper ever stops threatening that bread and slices it."

"I'll be in the study," Jason said. "Holler when you're ready."

Susannah sipped her coffee in the prolonged silence that frequently accompanied Pepper's displeasure. She put her elbows on the table and leaned her chin on her knuckles. "Okay, Pepper, what is it you're peeved about now?"

Pepper pursed her lips as she placed the bread, along with a crock of butter and a dish of preserves, on the table. "I was jest ponderin'," she said slowly, "since when do you need help saddlin' a horse?"

"Oh for goodness' sakes!"

"Don't pretend you don't know what I'm talkin' about. I been watchin' the two of you moonin' around, makin' cow eyes at each other."

Susannah bolted up, shoved her chair under the table and stalked out of the kitchen.

A half hour later she stopped at the door of the study. "Thanks anyway, Jason, for the offer, but I guess I better do it myself. Pepper thinks we're planning a tryst in the hayloft."

"Suit yourself. Use The Sullivan's saddle." His eyes started with her boots and moved slowly, lingering on her hips, over the fitted Levi's, then settled on the red plaid shirt where, buttoned low, it showed the line where the California tan stopped and the whiteness of her breasts began. "Not a bad idea," he said quietly.

Susannah opened her mouth to speak, but changed her mind, bent from the waist in a little half-bow as if acknowledging a doubtful compliment, then turned quickly and went out by the back hall.

She hummed tunelessly as she rode. Jason was right: even in a trot, Cindy was smooth. She leaned forward and stroked the horse's neck. "Let's go out on the old road, huh—see how you do in a lope."

Cindy responded immediately to a gentle nudge from the heels of the Justins and carried her rider down the dirt road, where the years dropped away and once again Susannah was the Apache princess escaping from the White-Eyes, taking the plan of ambush to her people in the Superstition Mountains. She was Jeanne d'Arc armed with the visions and the voices of saints, leading the French Dauphin's troops to victory in Orléans. She was Annie coming to Bill's rescue, popping off his captors with one perfect round. And she was the long-haired heroine in a white Desdemona gown, riding side saddle across the moors to one last meeting on the cliffs with her lean-faced, sad-eyed lover.

She reined in, smiling to herself, dismounted and rubbed Cindy's ears. "Good girl," she murmured, "sweet ride." Slowly, with her arms held behind her, she walked to the rail fence and looked out over the fields.

How far does it go, Grampa?
How far does what go?
This place.
As far as you can see.
I can see where the sky starts.
That's how far, Missy.
What's on the other side?

Nothing. Nothing worth bothering your head about.

And the *quiet!*

How long since she had stood alone in perfect stillness hearing only the sound of the wind, the sudden rustle of a rabbit, the thin cry of a hawk overhead. She added her own deep sigh to the pervading melancholy, then started off down the road on foot, the horse following.

The front porch still had an unused look, as if it had never known tall glasses of lemonade on hot afternoons or the red light of cigarettes inhaled in the gathering darkness, or observed fireflies or the moon rising over a bare shoulder. She tied the horse to a fencepost and walked slowly past the old car barn, still there but settling gradually into the earth, past the well and the smokehouse to the kitchen door.

It was almost noon when she heard him coming up the path. "Come on in, Jason," she called. "I've made some coffee."

"I saw Cindy—"

"I haven't used a wood stove for a long time—"

"I wanted to talk to you—"

"Everything looks just the same." She glanced up at him. "I recognize the curtains in the parlor—"

"Susannah. I need to say something."

She took two heavy white mugs from an open oilcloth-covered shelf, spoons from a glass on the table. "There doesn't seem to be any cream," she said.

He pushed back a curtain over the sink, pulled out a small can of evaporated milk and handed it to her. "You're bustling," he said. "Could we sit down?"

She punched two holes in the can of milk with an ice pick, poured the coffee, and they settled like uneasy visitors into chairs at opposite ends of the table.

"Feels almost like spring," Susannah said, in her best come-to-tea manner.

Jason sighed. "You're not much help," he mumbled.

"It didn't occur to me that you needed any help. If my memory serves me, you are a very articulate man." As she watched him turn his spoon over and over on the table, she realized that in spite of the tightness in her chest, the trembling hands that she kept carefully concealed in a bundle in her lap, what she felt was pure agonizing joy.

"I didn't mean it," he said finally. "I didn't mean what I said to you." She made a great show of looking puzzled as she savored the warmth of his discomfort. "What I said," he stumbled on, "that night you left."

She wrinkled her forehead as if trying to recall some long-forgotten detail. "It had to do, as I remember, with honor."

Jason nodded in careful agreement. "I thought it did. There was never a man who was a better friend to me than Gideon. You know how I felt about him. But what he asked was impossible."

The warm sensation ignited and burst into anger. "Under the circumstances, you mean," she said in a shaking voice. "Your honor was no match for an alley cat in heat." His face filled with pain as he reached across the table to her, but she leaned away from him, burying her fists deeper in her lap. "I remember one time," she went on, looking past him, "it was early summer and I was on my way to the stables when I heard it. That dry brittle rattle—there's no other sound quite like it, but you can't tell exactly which way it's coming from. I froze, still as death, then I saw it by the side of the path." She was looking directly at him now. "The tongue flicks in and out, trying to get a fix on your size, your position, maybe even your intentions. Who knows what goes on in that old brain? But dammit! God *damm*it, Jason, the fangs stay folded if you stay out of range. They seem so sinister, maybe they are." Her hands shot up from her lap and she punctuated her words with one open palm slapping down on the table. *"But they are fair!* You didn't even rattle, Jason. You sunk those words into me without any warning. I've still got the scars. Scars from decurved words. I branded myself with a fucking scarlet A, married a fag and then a womanizer. Pretty good punishment, huh? Atonement for having sex out of holy wedlock."

He eased out of his chair and moved slowly around the

table, his eyes never leaving hers, a contrite smile on his lips. His hand brushed her hair away from her cheek, and his fingers trailed down her neck and pushed aside the collar of her blouse. "You have a scar," he said softly, "that starts here and runs along the bone to the hollow in your neck. When you were ten years old you ran into the barbed-wire fence at the feed lot. I carried you up to the house, bleeding all over me." His hand moved down and stopped just below her waist. "And," he said, "you have an A—an A positive to be exact—on your left hip just below the dimple. But it's not scarlet, Susannah, it's a kind of royal blue. Your grandmother had it tatooed there so you wouldn't be given the wrong kind of blood if you were in an accident."

"Don't do that, Jason," she whispered.

"And you have a raised mole—light, almost golden brown—here just inside—"

Susannah brushed his hand away from her thigh, tripped as she scrambled up, and held on to the table for support.

He motioned with his head toward the parlor. "Have you forgotten that summer?"

"I haven't forgotten anything, Jason."

He ran his fingers through his hair and it fell forward as it had in dreams when his face had become indistinct pieces of features. "Neither have I," he said softly. "It was never as good with anyone else. Never. We had a lot of problems, but never in bed." A slow, mischievous grin spread across his face. "Or on the sandbar at the lake, or under the trees at the spring, or down by the creek, or out there on the front porch." He moved his fingertips lightly across her lips, touched her cheek and began again to trace the path of the barbed-wire scar. She closed her eyes and leaned against him, feeling a swelling sweetness like no other. She had waited so long.

Gently he led her toward the daybed in the parlor. She shook her head and pulled back.

"What's wrong?"

"The creek," she said, smiling. "Let's go down to the creek."

"It's chilly."

"I think it will be warm enough."

He crossed the room and impatiently jerked the comforter from the daybed. Then he laughed. "You still don't go in for beds, huh?"

He kissed her quickly, then took her hand and hurried her out the door, onto the path and to the post where Cindy stood. He eased the comforter onto the neck of the horse, untied the reins, mounted, then pulled Susannah up behind him.

She put her arms around his waist, her head on his back. "Are you going to make her rear up?" she said, giggling.

"We're riding to the creek," he answered. "Not into the sunset."

"I know, Jason. I know."

The creek turned at the big oak as it had that summer, but the water was low and sluggish and the tree's limbs were bare. Jason kicked the pebbles away and spread the comforter on the bank. He sat down, pulled off his boots, then stretched out a hand to her. "Hon?" He pulled her onto the soft down, fumbling first with his own buttons and zippers, then with hers. She shivered violently.

"What's wrong?" he asked.

"It's cold," she answered, moving closer to him.

He rubbed the gooseflesh under her open shirt, and his lips began to trace the scar toward her breasts.

"Tell me," she said. "Tell me again."

"Tell you what, hon?"

"How it's the best—the best with me."

"It's the best with you, Susannah."

"Why is it the best?"

He leaned back on his elbow and looked into her face. "Because you bring feasts in baskets, because you laugh and move and want it as much as I do."

"Did you love me?"

"You didn't used to talk so much."

"Did you love me?" she insisted.

"Of course I loved you. More than I have ever loved anyone." He reached for her again. She smiled and pulled away, pushed back the comforter and got to her feet.

Very deliberately, slowly, she buttoned her shirt and tucked it into her jeans, letting her eyes drift languidly over his flushed and puzzled face, and down the lean bare length of his body. Her tongue coiled around the years' carefully nursed rancor and pampered grudges, and the fangs unfolded. "That was a long time ago, Jason. There've been a lot of feasts in baskets since then. I've been under other trees, on other sandbars, watched the moon rise from other porches. With far bigger pricks than you."

FOURTEEN

BY SEVEN that evening, Pepper had given up trying to organize the household for supper; set out a cold buffet on the kitchen table and announced loudly that it was no skin off her nose if nobody was hungry and that she was going on down to her place to soak her poor tired feet. One by one, the children drifted into the kitchen, filled their plates and, since neither father nor mother was in evidence to inquire about the status of homework, gathered in front of the television set in the den.

Jason had not returned since he had left the house late in the morning, and Kate had been in the attic—asking not to be disturbed—since she and the children had come home from school. In her room, Susannah sat in front of her typewriter, sipping scotch and water, staring at a blank piece of paper. She had not expected that exhilarating moment of triumph to be so fleeting, or to be replaced—*ever* —by sharp twinges of regret, by the dull, nagging feeling that she had played a shabby trick, not only on him, but on herself.

She flicked the off switch on the typewriter and then, uncomfortable in the silence, turned on the radio. She picked up a book, put it down again, and stepped out into the hall. It was dark except for the slice of yellow light that shone from under the door to the attic. It had been hours! What on earth was she doing up there?

Aimlessly, she made her way down the stairs, poked her head into the den, where her greeting was barely acknowledged, that being a plea from Patrick, "Just a few more minutes . . ." She shrugged, went to the kitchen and made two chicken sandwiches and poured two glasses of milk. Even people who didn't want to be disturbed had to eat.

She knocked at the attic door. "It's me, Kate, I've brought you a sandwich. Okay?"

After a few moments, Kate opened the door. "I'm sorry," she said. "I didn't mean to hide out up here." She took the tray, set it down on one of the trunks that lined one wall, then turned quickly with a sudden thought. "I'm not taking anything. I mean, we'll sort through it all together. I just needed to . . ." She smiled wistfully. "I don't know what I'm looking for. Answers, I guess. But the phantom coming and going remains a phantom." With her toe she indicated the tidy stacks of envelopes on the floor. "If only I could think of her as this tragic but cheerful person who loved to travel and made lots of friends in exotic places and . . ." She paused and shook her head. "Maybe it isn't possible to see a parent, even an absentee one, as an ordinary person. Did the kids eat?"

Susannah nodded. "In the den watching television. They're a little uneasy about it."

"We're a bit disorganized, aren't we?" Kate picked up a sandwich triangle, one of the glasses of milk, and sat, hunched over, on a footstool. "I just can't sit in it," she said, motioning toward the rattan rocker.

Susannah stepped over the stacks of papers and sank down cross-legged on the floor.

"I've been thinking about what you said," Kate went on. "You know—if we had loved her more we could mourn her less? At first it made me angry. I told myself it was just another one of those pithy statements you collect. But then I started to think about it. I began to wonder about my own children, about what kind of tears, if any, they'll have for me."

"Nonsense. You're a very devoted mother."

Kate smiled wryly. "Efficient is more like it," she said, "and consistent. But I'll accept devoted—I need it." They smiled shyly at each other, and Kate sighed. "Well," she said, as if something had been settled, "at least there's one good thing about funerals. They can bring people—" she lowered her head—"families—closer." She raised her eyes and looked directly at Susannah. "I'm glad you're here."

Susannah clicked her tongue. "I'm surprised you'll have me. I certainly haven't been the guest most likely to be invited to stay anyplace. I can't figure out for the life of me why I carried on so about Father Flesher. I have this song and dance I do about birth control, and I really believe it! I really believe we're about to screw ourselves out of a planet to live on. But somehow, all that has nothing to do with a nice, understanding priest in Robina, Oklahoma, or with Momma." She lifted her arms in a helpless gesture. "Oh, I don't know why I was such a horse's ass!"

"Probably something to do with when you were here last." Kate flushed and began to clasp and unclasp her hands. "I am so very ashamed of the way I behaved."

"You weren't yourself, Kate. I know that."

"Then who was I? If it's true what you say, if the child I was is still a part of me, then surely that woman is still a part of me, too. I'm responsible for her. I'm accountable for everything she's done."

In the silence that followed there was the sound of a plane overhead, of muted television voices floating up from below, of distant music, and shallow breathing.

"Do you want to talk about it?" Susannah said finally.

"No. Yes. I don't know."

"You don't have to explain anything to me, Kate."

"I know. But I want to." She closed her eyes and spoke softly. "There was a terrible storm. I've never seen such rain. Most of the hands were away for the weekend, so I had to help Jason with the strays." She looked up, demanding understanding. "You know how I feel about horses.

Maybe it's some unresolved thing about Daddy, or one of those things I avoid because you do it so well. Anyway, Charlie shied and I went off. Jason had to get me in to see Billy, so he lost five or six head to the river. He said something—right there in front of Billy—about the little sister getting all the horsemanship in the family. He meant it as a joke, but there I was with a broken arm and a sprained ankle and him bellyaching about strays and nobody to help him, and I was fit to be tied. After we got home I really lit into him. I wanted to know what else you got all of, and I insisted straight out on knowing if the two of you slept together. Well, I was mad and he was mad and he told me a good deal more than I really wanted to know."

She paused and looked up, her face taut with pain. "Not only that you had but how good it was—how much better than . . . You see, I had lied to myself, had convinced myself I wasn't second choice. But there it was all out in the open—you had gotten there first. I couldn't pretend anymore. I was plain and dull and stiff, and the only reason he married me was for Grampa's land."

"He didn't say that," Susannah objected.

"No, he didn't say it, but I was sure it was true. I went to sleep with that thought every night and got up with it every morning." She took a deep breath and let it out slowly. "I went to a teachers' meeting in Kansas City that spring. I met a man there, a P.E. teacher from Nebraska, and I took him to my bed." Susannah reflected on her sister's choice of language, on the Victorian flavor of her confession. "I don't remember his last name."

"He's Hodge's father?"

Kate nodded. "He provided the sperm. There's more to fathering than biology."

"Does Jason know?"

Kate smiled bleakly. "Have you *looked* at Hodge? We've not spoken of it, but of course he knows. We've not quarreled either, not out loud, since that night. We're very careful to be polite and civil."

"Oh, Kate!"

"We haven't slept in the same bed for over a year, and we

haven't spoken of that either. One day I ordered twin beds from Martinsville, had ours moved into the sunroom, and the only thing Jason said was, 'which one is mine?'" She picked up another sandwich triangle and looked at it in a bewildered way, as if trying to determine what it was, then returned it very carefully to the plate. "This is all I ever wanted, to stay here on this farm, to marry Jason, to have a family. But it isn't a farm anymore, not like when Grampa was alive. It's a business now—big business. The children are more Pepper's than mine. They come to me for approval and—" she smiled like someone making a brave show of humor—"and syntax, but they go to Pepper when they hurt. And Jason . . . you've been gone for fourteen years, Susannah, and you still haunt this house."

Susannah shook her head vigorously. "That's not true, Kate. There's nothing here of me or of mine. You said so yourself and you were right. Don't you remember?"

Kate nodded and saw the vision of her sister standing before her, asking for the Meissen salt and peppers, asking for something of Gran, something of home to have with her.

No! They belong to me. All of Gran's things came to me.

I know that, Kate, but there's so much! Surely you won't miss an old cracked salt cellar and a pepper grinder.

They're mine. Everything in this house belongs to me. Bright Feather is dead! There is nothing here of yours. Nothing!

Susannah leaned forward and gripped her sister's arm. "I want you to listen, Kate, and I want you to hear what I say. I didn't leave Jason. Jason left me. The night Grampa died, Jason started to leave me, and I couldn't hang around and watch it happen. If you have lost him it's your own doing, nobody else's."

Kate spoke hesitantly, with physical effort, tears filling her eyes. "Pepper said he stayed home this morning. Did you—did you see him?"

Susannah arranged a deliberately vague look on her face. Be honest quietly, Marty had said, some of my cells are dying. Not a nonsequitur after all. "At breakfast," she said, "before I went riding." Then she grinned. "We had a long, erotic discussion about the weather." Kate looked away, embarrassed to be so well understood. Susannah pulled herself up, groaned and rubbed the calf of one leg. "I'll go perform a police action in the den, okay?"

Kate's voice stopped her on the threshold. "Missy?"

"Yes?"

"Thank you."

"That's okay. They're neat kids, I really enjoy them."

"That isn't what I was thanking you for."

Susannah bobbed her head, trying to think of something bright or casual or funny to say. It was so heavy, so formless and unwieldy, this burden of intimacy.

FIFTEEN

"I JEST don't like it," Pepper grumbled, settling herself uneasily onto her chair. "Meg, you ain't even touched your milk."

"Don't like what?" Jason asked absently. "Would you pass the biscuits, please, Patrick. What is it you don't like this time, Pepper?"

"The weather. It's too still, and so close a body can hardly get a breath down. They's a cyclone brewin' somewheres, that's what."

"Now, wait a minute, Pepper," said Susannah. "Everybody knows that Robina is tornado-proof. Don't you believe the stories about Gideon watching over the county?"

"You bein' Miss Smarty-Drawers agin, ain'tcha. Well, it jest may be that Gideon ain't payin' close attention. He may have other things to tend to."

Kate leaned across Susannah and patted Pepper's hand. "Now, you know we have the alert. If there's going to be a storm, we'll hear about it."

"I got my own alert," Pepper snapped, "and it ain't been wrong in sixty years." She narrowed her eyes and turned to Susannah. "They's all kinds of ill winds. Ain't none of 'em bode no good. Anyways, take a look at that old cat!" Pepper's long forefinger pointed imperiously toward the fireplace, where Iago huddled in the rocker, his paws folded under, his tail pulled tightly around his fluffed body. "Look at them eyes," she went on, "and see how pointed his ears is? He listenin'." She clucked softly. "They's an evil presence somewheres. Ain't you gonna eat your eggs, Hodgie? You cain't do your studies on biscuits and jelly."

Hodge poked dutifully at the scrambled eggs. "In assembly," he said, "Mr. Putnum said the alert system wasn't much good."

"He did not say that," Page objected. "Guy, you must be deaf. He said those airplanes the government sends to fly the weather during tornado season was a waste of the taxpayers' money."

"I am not deaf, Page, and I heard—"

"Boys. Boys!" Kate interrupted. "I think what Mr. Putnum said was that the alert hadn't been per*fec*ted, and that we need to know a lot more about the character of tornados before it could be."

"I'll tell you about its character," Pepper said. "It's the meanest, orneriest old wind ever was. It moves along God's earth, gobblin' up everything in its path and chewin' it up in its black jaws and spittin' it out again."

"Oh, Pepper!" Kate said impatiently.

"Is there really an alert?" Susannah asked.

"It's forecasting, actually," Jason answered briskly, not looking up, keeping his eyes trained on the biscuit he buttered. "The Weather Bureau tells us when conditions are ripe for a twister. The problem is, you can have the conditions and not have the twister or you can have the twister and not know you've got the conditions. In that case, the best alert is still somebody ten miles back down the road who sees it before you do and lets you know about it."

"That happened in Leedy," Kate said quickly, as she saw Pepper take another deep breath. "A telephone man sighted it before it got to town. He sounded the fire alarm, and all the volunteer firemen gathered in their usual spot, and the other people, as usual, came out to look for the fire. They announced over the P.A. system that it was coming, and when it got there almost everyone had made it to the storm cellars."

"It leveled the town," Jason added, "but there were only six lives lost." He paused and looked across the table at Susannah. "I suppose the alert is a good idea," he said solemnly, "but of course it has its limitations. It's a warning, kind of like the rattle on a diamondback, but you still have to have sense enough to get out of its way."

Susannah leaned forward and looked directly into his eyes. "There must be times when it goes off by mistake," she said. "Even a diamondback makes mistakes sometimes and rattles at something that isn't even there anymore."

Jason nodded thoughtfully. "Yes, I suppose you're right, Susannah. I guess that happens sometimes. I guess there's no such thing as a perfect communications system." He shoved his chair back from the table, rubbed his belly and smiled at Pepper. "Good breakfast," he said. "Say, why don't you and Iago turn on the radio and listen for the weather report. Not as much fun as communing with the spirits, but it's more accurate."

"That's *all* right," Pepper said, lifting her nose in the air. "Don't pay me no mind, I'm jest a crazy old woman!"

Kate got up from the table and took Jason's hat and jacket from the clothes tree by the door. "Will you be late?"

"No, we're checking the south fences today. I should be in around five or so."

There was an awkward silence, then Kate raised her face to him. He kissed her, smoothed her hair back, then playfully patted her behind.

"Have a good day," she said, coloring, pleased.

"You too." He rumpled the boys' heads affectionately, and kissed the milk off Meg's nose.

Susannah watched the scene of his departure over her coffee cup, feeling like an observer, an outsider who comes to the fire and is both warmed and made lonely by it. She knew, as surely as if she had watched it happen, that Jason had taken his passion—his rut, Pepper would have called it—home to his own bed; that they had made love in the night and probably the early morning. The evidence was there, in Kate's heavy-lidded eyes, her flushed face, and the languid, easy movements of her body.

The door closed behind Jason, and Kate turned her attention to the children, issuing admonishments about being late, instructions concerning teeth, faces and hair, as she finished her coffee standing up at the sink.

"I hope you're not bored," she said suddenly to Susannah. "There's so little excitement around here."

Pepper grunted loudly.

"I'm not bored, Kate," said Susannah. "I'm having a wonderful time."

"Good! Then we'll see you about three-thirty. Wonderful biscuits, Pepper, light as a feather! Please hurry, Patrick. How you do dawdle."

After the station wagon pulled away, Susannah became acutely aware of the quiet around her. "You're right, Pepper," she said, "it is still." The old woman sniffed, nodded and sipped her coffee. "Did you ever see one?" Susannah asked, as much to placate her as for the information.

"Two. The first in Louisiana. We didn't have no storm cellar, neither. But before my momma herded us kids into the ditch and covered us over with mattresses, I seen it comin' crost the field, dippin' its old black tail into the cotton and strippin' the ground bare. And they was the one when you and Kate was jest little fellers. It hit Newton, didn't set down here, but it spewed out hailstones as big as your fist." She thrust out her lower lip. "I didn't see that one. I don't know if it came from the Lord or was one that belonged to the Devil."

Susannah wondered if she had misunderstood. "Came from where?" she asked.

"They's the two kinds. The big fat one with the short funnel that's made in Heaven. The Lord sends that one down for wrongdoin' on earth. The other one with the long tail, that's Lucifer tryin' to git home, tryin' to git hisself home to his daddy. He commands the wind to start whirlin', then he makes hisself a ladder of lightnin' inside the wind, and he commences to climb. Ever' time he takes a step they's a great clap of thunder from above. That's the Lord shoutin' at him to git hisself back down where he belong. But he keeps on goin' so's the Lord takes up a handful of hailstones and He throws them right down the center of the wind."

Her eyes grew wider and she lowered her voice to a whisper. "That's when he does it! When the Lord strikes him with them hailstones, he drops down on the ground in a fury and he snatches up whatever's handy and he takes a big bite outa it and spits it out agin."

Susannah was trapped in the moment. "Why won't his daddy take him back?" she asked breathlessly. "Why won't his daddy let him come home?"

Pepper crossed her arms over her breast and stared at Susannah as through a window. "'Cause he ain't forgive him yet. He ain't forgive him for bringin' carnal knowledge to the garden."

Susannah felt the hair on the back of her neck bristle, and goosebumps appeared on her forearms. "I guess—I guess I better get to work," she said finally.

Lester sniffed the air like a hunting dog. He narrowed his faded eyes and stroked his whiskered face. "Jason, maybe we oughtta move the herd on over to the bottom."

"What for?" Jason answered.

"There's a storm comin' up. They'd be better off over there."

"Lester, you're as spooked as old Pepper. It'd take us three days to round them all up."

"No, sir. The Afriks are there already, and the others are mostly in the south pastures. I reckon we could get the lot of them over there in three-four hours." He sniffed again and nodded.

"Now, just what kind of information do you get from whiffing the air?"

"It smells heavy, don't go down easy. It's goin' to do something. Maybe just a lightnin' storm. I ain't sure what, but somethin'."

Jason rubbed his chin thoughtfully. "I'd planned to take

Kate to New Orleans this weekend. I wanted to see this job done before I go."

Lester shifted from one foot to the other. "It's probably nothin'," he said, "but just the same, there's somethin' kinda comfortin' about a valley—for man and beast."

Jason sniffed experimentally and shook his head. "Okay, Lester. I don't smell a thing but the slug of booze you had for breakfast, but we'll do it if you say so. Round up the boys and tell them to get a move on. I'd like to get home early."

Later, when they paused for a quick lunch at the shack, the men traded tales about the twisters they had seen or heard of. Jason listened with amusement to a vivid account of a cow swept up and away from the hands that milked her, carried aloft for three miles and deposited gently on the flat roof of a two-story building.

"Not a scratch on 'er, but she never gave another ounce of milk!"

Lester didn't join the others in laughter at the thought of a bewildered cow on a rooftop. "They do things like that sometimes," he said, "but mostly they just kill 'em—the folks and the animals and the crops and the towns." He ran his tongue along the cigarette he had just rolled. "I seen the big one in 'twenty-five. It came outa Missouri, moved crost Illinois and finally finished up in Indiana."

"Where'd you see it, Lester?"

"Town I was borned in, Murphysboro in Illinois. Funny thing about that one. It didn't have no tail atall, just a great blackness moving across the earth. They was two hundred and thirty-four people killed in Murphysboro, and three times that crippled up and hurt bad." He shook his head and hunched his shoulders around him. "I reckon I seen most of them folks, the dead ones and the maimed ones. I was lookin' for my ma, but I didn't ever find her."

The men were quiet for a long time, and then one of them spoke, hesitantly, respectfully. "That's a shame, Lester. That's a powerful shame."

Jason laid his hand on Lester's thin shoulder. Twelve years before, Lester had appeared at the door, a joyless solitary creature whom after a while Jason had assumed to be pastless. "I'm sorry," he said. "I didn't know."

"It ain't somethin' a person likes to dwell on, Jason, but it don't ever go away all together. There's somethin' about the way this day feels that brought it all back to me. Well—I'd say we'd best get movin'."

Page shifted uncomfortably in his chair. He fidgeted with his pencil and ran his finger around the soft collar of his sweater. Why had he worn a turtleneck, anyhow? Why was it so sticky, so muggy? And what did he care about Harry Emerson Fosdick and What Being a Real Person Means? What did he care about having a well-integrated life, whatever that was? How come they had so many stupid assignments? Why didn't they study about important things like space and stuff like that?

He sighed loudly and wrote: "A real person sees his duty and does it, regardless of the consequences. We cannot grow up to be good citizens with high moral standards unless we are truthful at all times with others and with our own selves."

He chewed on the yellow pencil. A lot of good it did to be truthful, to do your duty to high moral standards! He'd told Hodge about Mom so Hodge could see the world as it really is. The earlier you learned that, the better. But Hodge just shook his head and said he knew already. He said you had to remember that grownups were different than kids. They didn't see things so clear and sometimes they did things 'cause they couldn't help themselves. What kind of a stupid reason was that? And what was the use of reading a lot of stuff about how to be a Real Person if you couldn't grow up and do things like you wanted to, like you knew you should? What was the good of knowing what was right if you went ahead and did wrong?

He left the shaft of the pencil, now a mess of yellow flaked wood, and attacked the eraser, his lips drawn back from his square white teeth. Everybody knew what they called a woman that did things like that, a woman that did things like that with somebody else besides her husband.

He took his breath in sharply as his mind wandered over the edge into the center ground of the issue. If a woman who did that had a child, then that child was called a bastard.

Hodge raised his hand to be excused and received a silent nod from his teacher. He hurried past the boys' rest room and across the yard that separated the lower grades from the high school, entered his mother's classroom soundlessly and stood for several moments at the side of her desk before she was aware of him.

"Hodge! My, you startled me. What is it?"

"Could you drive me home at lunchtime, Mom?"

"Whatever for?"

"I'm worried about The Sullivan. I turned her out this morning, and with the storm coming up and all, she ought to be in the stables."

"Oh, she'll be all right, Hodge. She'll be right there at the fence waiting for you after school, just like always."

"But you know how she gets when it thunders—plain old loco crazy."

She shushed him gently. "What storm, dear? The sun is shining in a blue sky and you talk of thunder?"

"But Pepper said—"

"Hodge, Pepper is old and superstitious. We listen to her because she's dear to us, and in many ways she's very wise, but sometimes we have to separate facts from her fancies. Here, now, let me sign your note and you get back to class."

"I don't have a note," he mumbled. Reluctantly and in the face of his mother's raised eyebrow of disapproval, he turned to leave. "I wish you'd—"

"Son," she said quietly. "I called the Weather Bureau this morning. There is absolutely no sign of a front, no sign of turbulance, no sign of a storm. As a matter of fact," she added, smiling, "it looks to me like the sort of day when a boy rides out to meet his dad after school and does his homework later after supper. You suppose it's that kind of day?"

He returned his mother's smile in an attempt to acknowledge the offered treat, then left as quietly as he had come. Slow, unwilling footsteps retraced themselves across the graveled yard, through the hall, past the rest room, and then came to a halt outside the classroom. He wanted to believe the calm, reasonable assurances of his mother, but he was more finely attuned to the mystical prophecies of Pepper. The inner battle was brief.

From the silver-painted rack by the gym he took Ben Cochran's red-and-white Schwinn, and without a backward glance he peddled off down the blacktop road.

Susannah pulled a sheet of paper from the typewriter and placed it face down on another of its kind. She turned her head lazily from side to side, pushed her chair back on its hind legs and raised her arms in a great, long stretch. She turned the pages over and read them aloud:

Robina was born by accident in Oklahoma Territory in 1892. The birth was premature: Robina's founders were heading for California and unlimited prosperity. James Burns, a headstrong Scot who led the expedition, was prepared to reckon with hostiles, hunger, weather and any other hardship that might plague him on the journey. He was not prepared to reckon with an equally headstrong Scot, his wife, who set her slim foot down in the middle of the lush spring grass and refused to go one step farther.

They were alone the first year, this small group, but they never doubted for a moment that others would come. Others would sift the moist, fertile earth through their hands; would find shade under the green umbrellas of oak, maple and birch; would taste the sweet, clear water from streams abundant with silver bass and whiskered catfish; would stand quietly in the knee-high buffalo grass and hear the wind whisper, *this is home*.

The town was named for the Burns's youngest child, a thin, lovely girl with a mind fattened by her mother's love of learning. Now the town's oldest resident, Robina Edwards and time have served each other well. Last winter she fell and broke her hip, and after subsequent pinning was confined to a wheelchair for six months. Confinement, except by her own design, is foreign to her. Her spirit rebelled against it and in time began to long for the freedom of death. One night she awoke to the sweet singing of angels, and to discover flowers growing out of the wallpaper in her room. Her daughter, roused by voices, hurried to Robina's bedside and was admonished to watch her step, to walk with care through the fragrant meadow of blooming things.

The following night, when the vision appeared again, with songs more melodic and flowers more plentiful, Robina told it calmly that she had changed her mind, that she was not ready, that she would not present herself to her Maker with an unmended bone.

Susannah leaned forward on the typewriter and put her chin on her crossed arms. We could get some neat pictures of her, she thought, and a Grant Wood kind of thing of Mr. and Mrs. McKenzie. A shot of the old hotel, kind of tintypy, and a stark modern sort of thing of the school. The theme is progress and change. Progress without change. Why not? That they have a new schoolhouse and new cars and new methods, but old values. I suppose then you have to define progress. And how can there be TV sets and washing machines and no change in values? And what's wrong with change, anyway? Don't we have to change in order to survive? Isn't evolution itself a slow, constant upset of the balance of nature? On the other hand, maybe we survive by not doing anything different, by doing today exactly what we did yesterday . . .

She lit a cigarette, extended her arms wide and let them fall heavily against the sides of the chair. "Margaret Mead, you ain't," she said aloud. "Why not a simple story about the people here, how they live, what they believe in, what they hope for? God knows that's complicated enough."

She stretched again and wondering at the unseasonable heat, wiped perspiration from her forehead. Absently she looked around the room, and her gaze fell on the black photo album Kate had left for her. Maybe she could use some of that stuff. A nice touch—the town in the twenties, the thirties. And there was more of the same in the attic.

She picked up the album and began to turn the pages. "Me" was written in white ink under the cracked and yellowed picture of a baby in a crocheted hat and long white gown. "Me. Cousins Tim and Mary. Mama," under a trio of children in a wooden wagon pulled by a goat and followed by a tall, smiling dark-haired woman. "Grandfather Sullivan pitching horseshoes." "Me—Adam in Siloam Springs."

She turned the pages quickly, looking for early scenes of Robina: the old schoolhouse, the hotel with carriages and Model Ts in front of it. Suddenly she paused and then, slowly, began to turn back the pages.

Just then there was the sound of wheels on the gravel out front. She walked to the open casement window. "Hodge?" she murmured, closed the album and hurried out of the room, out of the house to meet him. "What's wrong?" she called from the porch.

He swung his leg expertly over the bar and braked the bike in a standing position. "Nothing, just a little worried about The Sullivan. I want to get her in the stable. She gets silly in a storm."

"Why didn't you phone? I could have gone after her."

"I thought about it, but I was afraid you wouldn't find her. I know where she goes. It won't take long." He hurried off toward the paddock, then turned and called, "Hey, Susannah, will you drive me back? I didn't have permission to come and I'd like to get back as soon as I can."

"Sure," Susannah said, cupping her hands around her mouth. "But hadn't you better let your mother know where you are?"

Hodge sighed and walked back toward her. "If I call her," he said, inclining his dark head, "she'd tell me to hightail it on back this minute. I can't do that. I'd have to disobey her twice and that'd mean a lickin' for sure."

"How do you know it's better for The Sullivan to be in the stables?"

He edged away from her, impatient to be on his way. He had no time for questions and answers.

"How do you know?" Susannah repeated, starting along the path after him.

He turned and spoke sternly. "I've got to go now, Susannah. I don't have time for any more talk."

Susannah watched him, admiring the graceful lope, the forward tilt of the body, until he disappeared around the corner of the stables. Whatever genes were mixed up in there, there was no question that was pure Warwick chin.

Patrick opened the brown paper sack with interest. "Egg salad," he said, unwrapping the wax paper from the sandwich. He lifted the corner of one slice of bread and peered inside. "With bacon."

"I gots peanut butter," his friend stated after a similar inspection.

Patrick shook his head negatively. "No peanut butter. What you got, David?"

"Mayonnaise and mustard," the boy answered.

"Trade you an egg salad, with bacon."

"What else you got?"

"Brownies."

"Nuts in 'em?"

"No."

"Okay. If you'll trade me the brownies for my sugar cookies."

"Are they lemony?"

"No, vanilla-y."

Patrick nodded, closing the deal, and Pepper's egg salad, the whites lovingly chopped into tiny pieces, the yellows rubbed through a sieve, mixed with crisp bits of bacon and homemade sweet pickles, was handed over in exchange for two pieces of Wonder bread glued together with Miracle Whip and French's mustard.

Patrick attacked his lunch in earnest and, when his mouth was quite as full as he could get it, said to his companions. "My folks talked about storms this morning at breakfast. Did your folks?"

"My ma was going to let me stay home, then my dad said everybody was to go on about their business."

Patrick went on between bites, "Dad said there was a tornado where most everybody was saved by the fire alarm. There was only six people killed."

"Six? That's a lot."

"Yeah," Patrick agreed, "but they were all old people. No kids. The kids all got in the same storm cellar and they stayed there for three days."

There was a momentary stoppage of chewing jaws. "With no grownups?" asked one of the boys.

"Just kids, and they didn't have anything to eat 'cept Hershey bars and Pepsi-Cola."

"And popcorn?"

"And popcorn."

"How would you brush your teeth? My mom'd be madder than an old settin' hen if I went for three days without brushing my teeth."

"Stupid! You can't worry about stuff like that in an emergency!"

"What happened when they got out, Pat?"

Patrick straightened and, using a jagged piece of celery to punctuate his words, said importantly, "Everything and everybody was blown away, so the kids had to build a new town all by themselves."

"I thought you said only six was killed."

"Yeah," Patrick said sadly. "The kids had to bury those and say prayers over them."

"But you said just six was killed. Where was the other grownups?"

"I told you," Patrick said, his voice rising, "they were blown away. They weren't killed, they were just blown away."

Five young minds briefly contemplated the prospect of a community where there were no adults to tell you to wash your hands, where you could eat what and when and where you wanted, where a school bell would never ring and you didn't have to spend precious summer mornings in Sunday school.

One of them spoke. "I guess it'd be okay for three days, but I wouldn't want my folks blowed away for always."

The others nodded in agreement, and they turned suspicious eyes on Patrick, who, taking a large bite of sugar cookie, complained in anguished tones that it was indeed lemony and that he'd been foully cheated.

"It ain't neither!" David said angrily. "My mom don't put lemon in her sugar cookies. You're just an old sourpuss, that's the matter."

"Yeah," said another. "You're just a troublemaker. You don't like your own folks, so you want everybody's folks to get blowed away."

"He shouldn't be in the Club," suggested another, and then announced, "Anybody who don't like their folks can't be in the Club."

Patrick blinked and lowered his head, avowing that he did so like his folks, but he hated lemon cookies and while he was at it, he hated the Club too. He stuffed wax paper, a half-eaten banana and a wadded napkin into his paper sack and sauntered with as much dignity as he could muster toward the door to the playground.

Meg poked along the short distance to Mrs. Satterlee's house, where, every day, she spent the time between the close of kindergarten and the last bell, when her mother and brothers would pick her up. Next year she would stay all day and learn to read and get loose teeth and everybody would call her Sarah Margaret, not Meggie—Meggie was a baby name.

She stopped to observe a basking horned toad and to inquire if it was lost. "Do you have a home, Mr. Horny Toad, huh? Do you have any brothers and sisters, huh? I have three brothers. I got an A on my letters. See?" She waved the piece of paper in front of the dozing reptile, which, in alarm, scurried off down the side of the road.

Meg sighed and said, regretfully, "Horny toads aren't like birds, birds have so much to say." And she shouted in the direction it had taken, "It's very good when you get an A on your letters. You can't just make them any old way. You got to follow the arrows."

She started to skip. "Follow the arrows . . . follow the arrows. . ." singing the words in a high, thin voice.

When she went to school all day and learned to read and was called Sarah Margaret, then she wouldn't go to Mrs. Satterlee's anymore. She wouldn't walk between the rabbit hutches and put her fingers through the wire to pet the soft pink noses. She would miss Mrs. Satterlee's house even if you did have to go outside to the bathroom. Everything in Mrs. Satterlee's house was in just one room, so if you wanted something it was right there. You could take a nap and wake up and have cookies and milk right in the same room!

Her father must be very rich, she reasoned, to have a different room for everything.

A sudden gust of wind took Meg's paper with its carefully formed letters, and lifted it high in the air and out over the field. She bounded after it, but stopped suddenly after several vigorous strides, surprised by the vicious whipping of wind around her. She shivered, and with a last look at the floating paper turned her footsteps to the west and Mrs. Satterlee's warm room.

She gasped at the sight of the sky before her, with its green-and-black clouds coming together and then pulling apart on the horizon. "The clouds are fighting," she whispered in awe, and for a moment she stood hypnotized by the roll and boil of the sky. Then terror replaced wonder, and Meg cried out, her shrill voice lost on the wind, "Mommy . . . *Mommy!*" And she ran, stumbling, sobbing, back toward school.

SIXTEEN

IT FORMED seven miles west of town, over Chester Barrett's potato field. Heavy, dark clouds moved over, under and around each other, bumping each other, swaying like giant drunken dancers, until they were glued into a thick, smoky mass. Then a wide, short funnel stretched toward the earth, and as if that were the signal, the cloud began to move forward.

Mr. Barrett, who lived alone, took time to collect his pipe and his dog and to telephone the school before he sought safety in his storm cellar.

Moving slowly, but in a straight and earthbound course, it traveled northeasterly, sucking up loose plowed ground, bushes, and full-grown trees into its belly. Where the Barrett property joined that of the Joseph brothers, the whirlwind became capricious, pulling itself up several hundred feet into the air and then swooping down on the Josephs' terrified sheep, striking and tossing some and lifting others out of sight, out of time.

It continued in a hopscotch pattern, pogo-sticking for the next four miles, toppling over a water tower, leaving untouched a sagging henhouse a few yards away, reducing to pitiful piles of lumber houses that had endured time's ravages for fifty years and more, leaving Ida Mae Anderson's clay pots of geranium cuttings for the knives of rain that would soon follow.

The funnel paused on the outskirts of town, took a disinterested jab at the Community House, and then descended in full fury down the main street. The green-and-white Conoco station on the corner of Main and Apple was the first structure hit, its concrete walls imploded, and brilliant blue lightning ignited gasoline from fallen pumps.

Next, it turned on the bank, then bounded against Perkins's General Store, which also housed the post office and the *Robina Herald*. Not a building on the north side of the street was left standing; few on the south escaped serious damage. In a matter of seconds, they were all rubble: wood splinters, jagged pieces of brick showing their clean pink insides, concrete chewed into powder. It pulled down three churches, scattering pews and altars over the streets and so disfiguring them that it was not possible later to sort them out properly, and it was in fact likely that when Robina was restored to order Methodist bottoms sat on Baptist wood.

In the A-1 Café, terrified lunchtime customers huddled in the walk-in icebox while the building was blown down around them. Only the abandoned hotel completely stood its ground. A relic from an age when Robina had entertained thoughts of growth and grandeur, it was built with pride and foot-thick concrete blocks, and even a wind such as this one found it unassailable.

Finally, the twisting pillar whirled across the highway, the railroad tracks, and, leaping over Mrs. Satterlee's rabbit hutches, bore down upon the school.

"The building, of course, is tornado-proof," the principal had said earlier in a wavering voice that convinced no one. "We're to open the windows and get all the children against inside walls." But Mr. Putnum was lately of Farmington, New Mexico, and the teachers home-grown. They would do it their way, the old way, with or without his permission.

Kate fought the urge to dash from her classroom, to find

and then to lead her own children to safety. She fought it and she hoped to God that the other teachers were as compulsively dutiful as she.

"In double file," she said loudly and clearly, holding up two fingers to emphasize her instructions. "Walk briskly but in order, and do not run until I tell you to." She spoke calmly, now and again biting her tongue to keep from screaming. "You, Stephen—lead the line out the west door and to the ditches. Briskly, now." She spoke words of warning and comfort to the children as they marched past her through the doorway, urging the laggers on with a hand placed firmly on their backs, falling in behind the last child.

Another line joined them as they turned the corner, and then another from across the hall. In a matter of seconds they had moved in her prescribed orderly fashion. "Now run!" she called when the last child had entered the play yard, and her heart leaped inside her as she watched the lines of children begin to emerge from the other building.

She looked wildly from one door to the other. Oh God! Should she go to Mrs. Satterlee's? But Mrs. Satterlee had a cellar, and surely she and Meg were safe inside it. How did one decide which child to look for first?

It was decided for her when Meg screamed from the parking area and Kate's eyes found her just in time to see the little girl fall, then scramble up again and run—a rolling, waddling run—toward her.

"Mrs. Garrity." It was Mr. Putnum, pale, trembling, but assuming with gallant effort the dignity of a captain who is losing his ship to the sea. "Mrs. Garrity," he shouted, "you should be with your class in the ditches. They're all out now. The classrooms are empty."

Kate nodded and opened her arms to gather Meg into them, kissing the bright tangled hair, murmuring her thanks into it.

"Mrs. Garrity!" the principal said firmly, as one speaks to another who has lost control.

"Yes—yes," she cried, her voice small on the rising wind. "Are you sure? Are you sure they're all out?" In answer, he crossed quickly to her, lifted Meg into his arms and, beckoning for Kate to follow, took off in a long-legged run toward the irrigation ditches.

Patrick and Page were there, barely recognizable for the mud that streaked their hair and faces. They crouched, with the others, in more than a foot of water, and Page, with a curious show of manners rather than relief, helped his mother into the ditch, reaching up to grasp her hands, then dropping them quickly when she tried to embrace him.

Kate kissed Patrick, then, holding both him and Meg to her, she looked to Page, her eyes blinking in a face that questioned and feared the answer in the same expression.

Page shook his head and yelled words that were lost in the wind. Kate, clutching the children, stumbled the length of the ditch until she found Iris McDonald. She grasped the woman's shoulder and shouted into her face. "Hodge?" There was no reaction. Kate cupped her hands and spoke into the ear that was turned to her.

"He left before lunch," Iris McDonald said, cupping her own hands. "Be-fore lunch," she repeated, speaking slowly and distinctly. "He asked to be excused . . . *to be excused . . .*"

"Oh my God!" Kate cried, and tears of desperation stood like great pools in her eyes.

"I thought he was probably ill . . . *ill*," Iris McDonald replied.

And Kate shouted into her ear, angrily, louder than necessary, "Why didn't you report him?"

"Report Hodge?" The other woman looked puzzled.

Kate pressed her children against her trembling body and eased into a froglike crouch. The noise was deafening; surely these were the same sounds as at the end of the world when the earth would hurtle crazily out of orbit toward some unknown collision.

Standing apart from them, Page heard it as a host of chariots traveling at top speed across the sky. He peeked over the edge of the ditch and watched in horror as the advancing tower of spinning debris lashed out at the school. It was just as Pepper said: it chewed up things in its terrible jaws and spit them out again. But God wouldn't let something so awful happen unless He was angry, unless somebody made him mad enough. Like when there was the Flood, and the locusts and the toads, and people made into pillars of salt. He stared out, paralyzed by his own thoughts, into the blackness. Could his mother be that bad? That powerful? That she could cause this to happen?

While he wrestled with images of his own making, the dark column appeared to stamp an unseen foot and to move on with renewed vigor away from the school, north and east across the fields.

Toward home.

Susannah jumped up from her chair at the sound of Pepper's screams from the downstairs hallway, and rushed to the railing to find the old woman looking wild-eyed up at her, Iago dangling in the crook of her arm.

"It's comin'," Pepper shrieked, in a voice that proclaimed the Day of Judgment. "It's comin', O dear Lord Jesus! We gotta git to the fruit cave—"

"But Hodge—?"

"We gotta git to the fruit cave," she repeated. "Crack the windows upstairs. Hurry, child—hurry!"

Susannah did as she was told, dashing from room to room. She started down the stairs, then ran back for her shoulder bag, the typewriten pages, and, as an afterthought, she scooped up the black album.

On the front porch the rising wind plucked the screen door from her hands and flung it against the green swing. She hurried down the porch steps, crouched and shouted for the dogs. Blue came quickly and huddled against her. Poking her head through the hole in the lattice, she could see Timothy, one. paw raised in indecision, flanks quivering. "Come on, Tim," she called. "Come on, boy." The brown-and-white form slunk forward, unconvinced, unwilling. As he approached the opening, she reached out for his collar, and he jumped back, wagging his tail in apology. "Come on, Tim—oh, please come," she implored through clenched teeth, forcing sweetness into her voice. The dog whined, licked her outstretched hand, and allowed her to take hold of his collar.

With one last searching look toward the east, the direction Hodge had taken, Susannah lowered the heavy cellar door into place.

Pepper had lit the lantern, and in the dim glow Susannah could see her, motionless on her knees, her head bowed on clenched hands. "Pray for them, Susannah," she said quietly, not raising her eyes. "The good Lord will hear our prayers and keep them safe."

"This has nothing to do with God," Susannah answered in a strained voice.

Pepper looked up. "Everthing has to do with God," she said, and bowed her head again.

As Susannah paced up and down the length of the cellar, stopping to stroke Blue's ears, to speak softly to the shivering Timothy, the sounds began to come to her. They crept through the solid cellar door, traveled as easily through the earth as seeping rain. A monstrous swarm of bees, an unholy flock of birds, the bellowing and panting of creatures seen only in dreams—assailing, devouring the land. She could hear it only in metaphor, it was too alien, too awful to hear as itself.

Without any clear awareness of what prompted it, she started up the ladder, but Pepper's outcry checked her. "I've got to see," she said, hissing the words through her teeth.

"No!" Pepper cried again. "Here! See it here!" She came up from her knees, went to the center of the cellar and peered into Gideon's homemade periscope. Moments later she dropped her hands to her sides and turned limply away. "It's the Lord's," she wailed. "It's the Lord's avenging wind."

Her eyes were bright nuggets as she crossed swiftly to the ladder and dragged Susannah roughly down off the rungs. "Did you do this?" she shouted, her breath hot and dry on Susannah's startled face. "Did you lay with your sister's husband?"

Susannah squeezed her eyes shut and shook her head rapidly back and forth.

Strong, clawlike fingers held her shoulders in a vise. "You tell me the truth, Susannah! You hear me? Did you lay in sin with your sister's husband?" And she shook her with a fierceness that caused the tightly shut eyes to open into round, frightened circles.

"No!" Susannah cried, pulling out of Pepper's iron grasp and staggering back to the ladder.

Pepper came after her, catching hold of her shoulder again and swinging her around. "Do you swear it?"

Susannah nodded slowly, taking hoarse, ragged breaths with each downward movement of her head.

"Say it," Pepper cried. "Say you swear!"

"I swear it," Susannah whispered.

Pepper watched her for a long hushed moment, then reached out and lightly touched Susannah's face. Tears were running down her cheeks as she turned with slow, heavy steps back to the periscope. She wiped her eyes on her apron, squinted into the periscope, moving it in a full circle, then looked away. Again she sank onto her knees and bowed her head, and her body began to rock back and forth. Susannah knelt beside her, held on to her broad shoulders, and leaned heavily against her. Rocking with her, back and forth.

"It's what I feared," Pepper moaned. "He come for Gideon. He come for Gideon at last."

Susannah shuddered, and said gently, "Grampa's dead, Pepper. Remember? Grampa's dead."

"He come for Gideon's house. Gideon's sin is visited on his house." Still rocking, Pepper began to weep.

Susannah felt an eerie coldness settle around her. It was quieter now; the swarms, the flocks, the nightmare creatures had moved on, leaving only the sound of rain dully striking the cellar door. She looked closely at Pepper's wet face, shining in the flickering light from the lamp.

"What sin, Pepper? What was Gideon's sin?"

Fragments from the unrelenting past came spilling out. Gideon, the paragon, the fairest, the noblest, the most just and merciful of all men, had sent Elizabeth from his house, had taken her children from her by legal but shameful means. To save them from the worship of idols. To lead them in the path of true righteousness. For his name's sake.

"Pepper, I don't understand what you're saying. What did Gideon *do?*"

"He tempted your momma with thirty pieces of silver—"

"You mean he paid her to leave us? He *bought* us? I don't believe it! Gran wouldn't have let him do a thing like that."

"Evelina didn't know. It was between Gideon and Lizbeth. He give her money for all her life and she was not to come back here 'cept to visit. Thirty pieces of silver. She signed a paper with the lawyer, Mr. Apperson."

"But didn't she even try to keep us? Didn't she stand up to him at all?"

"Now, you know there was nobody to stand up to your granddaddy when he had his mind settled on a matter."

"So she just took the money and split, just like that! She wasn't even strong enough to fight for her own babies."

"Oh Missy—Missy! Your poor momma was jest a baby herself, still mournin' your daddy. She did the best that was in her to do. You understand that? She made a bargain with Gideon's devil and she kept her part of it, even after he was gone."

Pepper heaved a heavy, long sigh, patted Susannah on the shoulder and rose with effort from her knees. "You let her be, Missy," she said sadly. "Let your momma be."

In the rain of mud that followed on the heels of the wind, Kate stumbled up and down the long ditch, and then over the fields behind the school, questioning everyone, moving away impatiently as they told their stories, calling Hodge's name over and over until at last it became a low croak lost in the clatter of the rain.

The order that had characterized flight from danger dissolved into chaos when the danger had passed, when the damage was done. Dry-eyed, tight-lipped men and women moved like disturbed ants over the field, down the road,

calling their children's names in raspy voices, weeping un-
ashamed when they found them.

The principal from Farmington had been correct. The
walls of the new schoolhouse were tornado-proof. But the
vast expanse of modern, sliding plate glass was not and had
produced a mammoth shower of crystal daggers that were
embedded in walls, floors, desks, and ceilings.

Kate wandered from one shell of a room to another, gripping Meg's hand so tightly that the child finally cried out.

"I'm sorry, darling," Kate said, her body relaxing with
the acceptance of what she had tried to deny. "I guess he
must have gone after The Sullivan. We better see about the
car. We better get on home."

The twister had skipped over the parking lot. Only paint
was damaged—pitted, peeled and eaten by flying glass,
covered with thick sheets of red-brown mud.

"Look," cried Meg, pointing to the ground. "It's my
friend."

"Come on, dear," Kate said, pulling her along.

Meg wrenched free and ran back. "The wind hurt my
friend," she said, and she cradled in her hands the small
limp body of a horned toad.

The devastation along the way was at once complete and
perfunctory. On the north side of the road, the whirlwind
had knocked down fences, uprooted trees and trampled the
dry winter stubble in the fields. On the south side, the land
slumbered, untouched, undisturbed.

Meg cooed quietly to her lifeless charge, her young mind
protecting itself from only half-realized fears of what they
would find at home. Patrick sat beside her, straight and
rigid as a perfectly formed stick. It wasn't the same when it
happened. It wasn't the same as just talking about it. In his
mind, he went over the story again and again, trying to
separate out his parents' original telling from his own em-
bellishments. The people weren't really blown away; there
wasn't really anybody killed; nobody buried and no prayers
said over them. His dad was really okay, safe in the shack

or under one of the big trees in the bottom. And Hodge was home right this very minute waiting for them to come . . .

"I can't see the road," Kate complained as she leaned forward over the steering wheel, trying to find the edge of the blacktop in the downpour.

"It's your fault!" Page blurted out the words as if unable to hold them in his mouth a moment longer.

She took her eyes from the road briefly and looked questioningly at her son. "What's my fault?"

"All of it! In the old days you would have been stoned!"

And Kate felt as if she had been. The breath was knocked from her as surely as if he had used, instead of words, a rock or a fist or a club. Slowly, carefully, not trusting the wheel in her shaking hands, she brought the car to a stop and turned to face him.

He pounded his knees with his open palm. "I know!" he cried. "I know about you!" The pounding stopped abruptly, and he went on, his voice cold and even. "I told Hodge. It was my duty to tell him."

An enveloping sense of relief came over her. She breathed deeply and whispered, "Your duty?" And her mind's eye produced a montage of nastiness she too had done in the name of duty, superimposed on a portrait of the young Kate, advising her grandfather in a left-handed, unsigned message that Susannah had been locked out of the dorm, calling it a moral obligation, denying the gut-eating envy that prompted it. She reached out to her son, shaking her head sadly, "So like me. . ." He drew away from her, dropping his head so that his chin almost touched his chest.

What she wanted most, in the deepest part of her, was to hit him. To hit him hard across his sullen, pouting face. Instead, she rested her hand on his shoulder, and he let it lie there.

"Page?" she questioned softly.

After a moment he turned his head toward her but did not meet her eyes.

"He isn't even his son," he said, his face contorted in a tragic mask, "and he's the favorite. It isn't fair."

"Oh, Page!" she cried out, feeling his pain as if it were her own. She glanced behind her and lowered her voice under the rain. "I've spent most of my life picking and gnawing at feelings like that. It ruins things. It ruins everything. The same thing can happen to you."

"I'm not like you," he said in sharp protest, and she let her hand fall limply from his shoulder.

She slid back across the seat and sat quite still, staring blankly through the window into the gray void that surrounded the car. "You have to forgive me, Page," she said finally. "Not for my sake, but for yours."

He met her eyes now. "Does Dad know?"

"Why?"

"Because it's his right to know. If you don't tell him, I will."

She smiled grimly as she listened to him experiment with emotional blackmail. "He knows," she answered, and watched his rising confidence fall into disbelief.

"And he goes on living with you?"

"It was years ago. I was sick. I was sick with the same kind of jealousy and self-righteousness that you have now. I carried it around with me like a precious burden." She sighed, then once again reached out to touch his shoulder. "You were conceived in love, and you were carried with more joy than I have ever known, before or since. Oh, Page! There are no favorite children, only different children. Each one cherished for the difference." Slowly she moved her hand to the gearshift and eased the car to the center of the road.

In the back, Meg sang in a high, thin voice, dirgeful, heartful, and out of tune, to the accompaniment of the windshield-wiper metronome, mixing up the familiar requests and expectations: "Jesus loves me yes I know yes I know I pray the Lord my soul to take for the Bible tells me so *yes I know yes I know yes I know* . . ."

She drove into the yard, slowly and carefully to avoid the scattered branches, severed trunks and uprooted stumps of pecan trees. "You'd best stay in the car," she said gently, turning to the younger children, hoping to protect them, at least for the moment, from what might be out there. And to Page: "Come with me, son—please." But he was looking past her in openmouthed astonishment at the sight in front of him.

Susannah, her hair wet against her head, her clothes soaked through, stood like a bedraggled sentry in front of what had been the house. The kitchen fireplace still stood, pointing its chimney like a lonely accusing finger to the sky. All around it lay the ruin of years—Gideon's house, a living thing because of what had happened within its walls, now dead.

"Are they here?" Kate called, running toward Susannah.

Susannah shook her head. "We just came out of the cellar, just now. Pepper's gone on over to her place."

"Hodge—?"

"He went after The Sullivan. I'm sorry. I should have stopped him. I was about to go look for him now. I thought Jason might—"

"Jason was going to the south fields." Kate pointed toward the north, moving her finger up and down in her excitement. "The wind went the other way, you can see its path."

Susannah put her arm around her sister's shoulders. "Why don't you get the kids on over to Pepper's. It's the only thing left standing—and the stables. I'll ride out and look for Hodge. I'm sure he's all right, Kate—I'm just sure of it! Probably he's already found Jason and they're on the way home right now."

"I'll go with you," Kate said quickly. Susannah's jaw dropped in surprise. "Unless there's a faster way," Kate said impatiently, reading her sister's face. "He's my *son!*" She turned toward the car and motioned for Page to follow. "You get the horses ready," she said to Susannah. "I'll be right back."

As she started off in a run, Page caught her arm, and she whirled to face him. "You go on, Mom," he said softly. "I'll look after Meg and Patrick."

Even in the driving rain it was an easy trail to follow. The funnel had trampled and uprooted the grass, and cut a swath they judged to be four or five blocks wide across the field. They reined in on the gentle rise that separated the near from the far pasture, and turned to look down on the corpse of the house.

"He would have seen it from here," Susannah said. "He would have seen it in time to get out of its way."

"If he could tell which way it was going," Kate said grimly. She looked first to the right and then the left, straining to see through the wall of rain that beat down on them. She raised her arm and looked questioningly at Susannah, who nodded in agreement, and they urged their horses into a trot in the direction that offered the most hope.

"How is it in town?" Susannah asked.

Kate answered without looking at her, squinting her eyes, craning her neck, and moving her head in a slow alert arc from side to side. "I was looking for Hodge, so I didn't really talk to anybody—just heard pieces and snatches. Billy's setting up in the old hotel. I told him we'd be back to help just as soon as . . . just as soon as we could."

"Was anybody. . ."

"Marylouise's mother. Mr. McKenzie. Nat Apperson." Her voice had a curious sound to her, a deadpan quality, as if she could not afford to feel the impact of her own words. She reached across the space between them. "Bruce Boggs. We went to school together. He was in his car on the road just west of town. They think he must have rolled down the window and stuck his head out to look around. They haven't found it . . . but there was the rest of him—sitting there behind the wheel. Oh God! There's no sense to it!"

Minutes later they made out the dim forms of horses and riders in the distance. "Jason!" Kate shouted. "Jason! Hodge!" And careless of the slipping, sliding mud, she kicked the horse into a run.

"Is everybody all right?" Jason called.

"Hodge?" Kate cried out.

GIDEON'S HOUSE · 193

"Isn't he with. . .?" Susannah added, her words trailing off into question marks as she searched the faces of the men.

Clumsily Kate climbed off the horse and stumbled toward Jason. He swung down and took her into his arms. For the barest fraction of a second she gave thanks. If they were to grieve, it would be together. "He went after The Sullivan," she told him in a choking voice. "Where does The Sullivan go?"

"She sometimes grazes in the north pasture," Lester said slowly. "But she don't go far from home as a rule."

Jason's face was ashen. "Lester, you ride the north fences. Jimmy, you and George take the lower fields. The rest of you scatter out in the south. We'll make a circle near the house. Whoever finds him, fire three shots. Come on, Kate, Susannah."

They retraced the route the women had taken and returned to the rise. Jason took his breath in suddenly when he saw the house, but he made no comment. He asked about the others as they rode, and listened gravely while Kate told him about Hodge leaving school, reached over to reassure her when she took the full blame for it. "He was right," she said, "the stables weren't touched." Then she told of the other children, of the town, of Bruce Boggs and Mr. McKenzie.

"The herd?" Susannah asked.

"The herd?" Jason repeated in a distracted way.

"The cattle? Are they all right?"

"Oh yes—yes," and he dismissed them absently.

She didn't want to tell him, but they were all making such an effort to set things out as they were, to get the worst over with. "The barn was flattened," she said, "and the chain link scattered everywhere, but I couldn't find any sign of the gaur."

"He would have ridden the fences," Jason said suddenly and changed the direction of his horse. "You say he left school before noon?" Kate nodded. "So he had more than enough time to find her before the wind came up. All he has to do is whistle for that horse and she comes to him. But he didn't know we were moving the herd, so he would have looked for me along the south fences."

They rode in silence for the next quarter hour, Susannah from time to time casting a covert eye toward Jason, wanting to reach out and wipe the rain and the worry from his face. To cry, to shout, to plead that she was sorry, heartsick sorry. So much time wasted in meanness, in smallness, in getting even, in wounding and setting up to be wounded, in beating to death the roses. For what? When they were so fragile anyway?

He pulled up and turned to face them. "He wouldn't have come this far," he said heavily. "If he had, he would have seen us. Let's go back." They turned their horses, and at that moment the sound of a shot jarred the air. They stopped and waited for the two that were to follow. No more. A single shot, echoing through the shallow valley. Jason kicked his horse hard in the flanks, and the horse, after a whinny of protest, plowed up a narrow ravine.

Lester looked up at the sound of their approach. Jason swung down and ran to where Lester stood, the gun still in his hand. "I knowed you'd want to do it, but she was in a poor way. She couldn't wait."

The muscles in Jason's jaw worked convulsively. "Hodge?" he questioned.

Lester shook his head. "That boy wouldn't leave no animal in pain 'less he had to. It may be he went to the shack for a gun." Jason nodded and turned away.

Susannah knelt beside Bright Feather's colt, all that was left here of her legacy. The distinctive Appaloosa pattern was blotted out with a mixture of blood and mud as the rain flowed over but did not wash the body. Splintered white bone protruded from the right front hock, and there was an ugly gaping gash along the crumpled ribs. Susannah stretched out her hand and touched the soft, dark nose, still warm, just moments from life. Jason took her arm, and she struggled up and leaned against him.

"There!" Lester cried out. "There's somebody on foot!"

He came toward them in a limping, sideways run, one arm dangling in an odd way, a rifle held in the other. When

Jason started toward him, Hodge stopped, knowing it had been done. Neither spoke. Jason held him carefully, mindful of the arm.

Finally Hodge said, in a dull, tired voice, "We would have made it, but the bay ran off and we tried to catch her. We were out of the path of it, but the bay ran off."

"I know, son, I know."

"Is everybody okay?"

"Everybody's okay."

"I shouldn't have come. I'm sorry, Mom—you told me not to come. Probably The Sullivan would have made it on her own."

Kate laid her cheek against his rain-plastered head. "You did what you thought was best, that's all any of us can do. Oh, I'm so sorry, darling."

Hodge looked past her to where the others stood in a silent circle. He swallowed hard. "Did you. . .?"

"No, son," Jason answered gently. "Lester did it."

Hodge lifted his face. "You told us nothing really dies. You said everything becomes a part of something else." His eyes started to fill and his lips trembled. "Is that all? Isn't there something more?"

SEVENTEEN

THE RAINFALL stopped in the early evening, and the front moved off to the east. The twilight sky was scrubbed and clear, and Chester Barrett noted that at least the search parties would have a moon to do their work by.

The Salvation Army from Martinsville was the first outside group to arrive. They brought urns of coffee, sandwiches, doughnuts, blankets and words of comfort. The Red Cross unit from Tulsa came soon afterward and was headquartered with Billy in the hotel, where they worked by flashlight and kerosene lamp. Ambulances screamed in and out of town, carrying the badly injured to the hospital in Martinsville and, when it was full, to Tulsa. The people with lesser hurts of cuts, bruises and bewilderment were cared for in the lobby of the hotel, and those who no longer needed Billy's attention were laid in neat rows in what had once been the hotel dining room. There were names printed on white cards and pinned to the blankets that covered them. On some there were no cards.

The last rescue party, the one led by Jason Garrity, returned to the hotel shortly before midnight, by which time power had been restored, fires had been put out, and two dairymen from Martinsville had arrived with barrels of drinking water. Within twelve hours after the tornado hit, Robina had begun the long slow process of recovery.

Chester Barrett, notebook in hand, stopped Jason on the hotel steps. Chester, a retired journalist, was a man whose world made sense to him only when he had a count on things. He added Jason's grisly findings to the list he was compiling, which brought the totals to twenty-three dead, nineteen of those positively identified, seventy-four seriously injured and removed to hospitals, sixty with superficial wounds, and at least seven unaccounted for.

By Chester's rough calculations, the twister had moved at a speed of twenty miles an hour in an east-by-northeast direction. Traveling that slowly and cutting a path only an eighth of a mile wide, it was by Weather Bureau standards a moderate storm. The amount and extent of damage was not high when compared, for example, with Blackwell and Udall. But then, Chester was quick to point out, loss, like gain, was a relative thing.

He wanted to know, for the record, and while it was still clear in Jason's mind, what it looked like in the east part of town where he and his group had been digging.

If there was a trademark, Jason said, it was the kindling. Everywhere you walked over the spongy ground, you walked on slivers and sticks of kindling. Pieces of wood that once were a child's bed, a dining-room table, a roof, a wall, a floor; the pieces of wood men put together to make a home. Death was obscene. Here, smashed into the wet ground, were half a dozen chickens, gutted and picked as clean as if they'd been scalded for broiling. A dead black cocker lay on a clean, waxed oak floor of what had been a house. A child's toy road-grader sat under some kindling on a sidewalk, its blade spattered with mud, as if it had been working. You walk and walk and step over the fallen electric wires and around the uprooted bathtubs and over the endless piles of kindling. You dig where you think you see movement, where you think you hear sounds. But you can't focus your mind on any single, exact description of

what it looks like. You walk and you dig and you wonder.
Why? Why here?

Susannah bent over the toilet in the old-fashioned ladies'
room of the hotel. Her hands clutched the sides of the
bowl, and her empty stomach responded with dry wretch-
ing. She coughed and reached up with a blind palm for the
chain. She had just watched a man die. She had seen animals die both from violence and from time; she had seen
seasons die and had mourned them in abstract understanding of her own destiny; she had never before watched a
human being die, and she was sick with the finality of it,
with the lack of dignity, and most of all she was lonely for a
lost faith to transcend it.

The worst thing was that he had known, and he had
fought against it, grasping her hand in an effort to keep
from going, holding it so tightly she felt her knuckles being
ground together. He had called for someone, over and over;
Lila? Leah? She couldn't make it out. His wife? His sister?
Someone as familiar as his own bones, as comfortable as the
old green sweater he wore, someone broken in and necessary. She had sent Page out into the streets to look for Lila,
for Leah, but he had returned alone. The man had to settle
for a strange and alien hand. She would have liked to do
that for him, to find that necessary person to help him die.

When the blood gushed forth from his mouth, welling up
from someplace vital and violated, she wiped at it and cried
desperately for Billy. The blood stopped and the breath
with it. The hand still gripped hers.

She reached again for the chain, pulled it, and struggled
to her feet. There was a light tapping on the door. "It's
open," she said, not bothering to lift her head, watching the
water swirl down.

Kate put her arm around her sister and led her out into
the lobby. "You've had such a time," she murmured. "That
poor man. No one knows him, he must have been driving
through. Here, sit down for a minute and get your bear-
ings. I'll get you some tea. That'll settle your stomach."

Kate moved briskly across the lobby and returned moments later, a steaming mug in her hand.

"Thank you," Susannah said, forcing a smile, her eyes dark smudges in her pale face. "I'm better now."

"When you've rested, had your tea. . ." Kate paused and pointed to the center of the room. "One of the little Anderson girls. Not hurt, but very frightened. Her folks haven't turned up yet. And the boy next to her, cuts and abrasions. Would you see to them?"

Susannah nodded, set the cup down on the floor and began to look wildly about her. "The album? Where's the album?"

"What album? Are you all right, Susannah?"

"Momma's little black album. I had it when I came in— it's with my jacket and my bag."

"Now—now," Kate said soothingly, "we'll find them when we finish."

"No! Now! Where'd I go first? The Morley girl . . . where is she?" Susannah whirled around the room, searching under tables and chairs, and finally, crawling on her hands and knees, found the album under one of the cots. She lifted it in the air and waved to Kate across the room.

Kate started toward her with a heavy, sinking feeling. It had been too much for her sister. She should have sent her home. "Listen," she said, speaking softly. "Hodge is back from the hospital. Do you feel like driving him home?"

"Have you looked at this?" Susannah said, holding out the album.

"I glanced through it. Susannah, dear, I have work to do now. We'll look at Momma's album together when we get back."

"Goddammit, Kate, quit treating me like a loony. Look at this!" She turned the pages quickly, found the one she was looking for, and thumped it with her forefinger. "Who is that? Who is that man?"

Kate sighed. "Well, it's written right here, it says it's Grandfather Sullivan pitching horseshoes. It's Momma's grandfather."

"Look at him!"

"Susannah, please lower your voice."

"Look at him," Susannah repeated in a loud whisper.

As Kate gazed at the picture, deep furrows appeared in her brow.

"Who is it?" Susannah demanded.

"Oh dear God!"

"It's Hodge! Do you see that? The very image!"

The album slipped from Kate's grasp and she held on to Susannah for support. "Oh dear God."

Susannah grinned broadly. "I hate to have to be the one to explain the facts of life to a biology teacher, but I guess I've had more practical experience than you have. Listen. Just because you sleep with a man, that doesn't necessarily mean he gets you pregnant." She paused, smiling thoughtfully to herself, then added, "And it doesn't mean you have to carry his sperm around in your head for the rest of your life, either."

"Oh God, what'll I do?"

"For once, for *once*, what you'll do is let God off the hook. This is your mess—you clean it up. *Tell* them."

Kate shook her head violently. "I can't do that," she moaned. "I just can't do that."

Susannah looked at her for a moment, then stooped to retrieve the album and brusquely tore out the page containing Grandfather Sullivan. "Frame it!" she commanded. "Hang it on the wall. Let the old horseshoe pitcher do the talking." She took a deep breath, blew it out and said, "Okay, where's the Anderson girl?" Kate pointed toward the center of the room in a dazed, uncertain way. Susannah took a few quick steps, stopped suddenly and spoke over her shoulder. "By the way, Sister Kate, I think you have grossly overrated your sins."

It was after one. Susannah sat on the edge of Marie Anderson's cot, telling the little girl that it was time to sleep now, smoothing back her hair, making soft, unconnected sounds that grew into an old foolproof lullaby her grandmother had left in her mind.

She sensed, rather than saw, someone looking at her, and when she turned her head she found him standing, one hand in his pants pocket, at the foot of the cot. As familiar as her own bones, broken in, necessary.

"I hoped you would come," she said.

"I got here as soon as I could," he answered.

"Would you do something for me, Marty?"

He smiled anxiously and sat on the cot beside her. "Anything," he said.

"Would you hold my hand?"

At five after four Billy thanked his volunteers and told them to go home and get some sleep. "If you don't have a home," he added wearily, "then go to the Community House. There's plenty of bedding there. And food and water." He lowered his eyes. "And neighbors."

The blue, pre-dawn light, like a pale myopic eye, was kind to the house. Jason slowed the car as they drove by it. Kate shuddered and turned her head away. Smoke beckoned from the chimney of Pepper's house on the other side of the stream, and they opened the door on the smell of baking ham and rising bread.

"You folks wash up," Pepper greeted them. "I'll git breakfast on." She smiled and bobbed her head at Marty. "I figured you'd come back."

Marty smiled back out of his red, exhausted eyes, his face streaked with dirt. "Had to, Pepper, ran out of pickles."

"Good thing he did," said Jason, beaming newfound respect on the polo player from Hollywood. "He put himself in charge of lost souls. Even found Melinda's collie."

Susannah sank into a chair and surveyed Pepper's white, enamel-top table, set for a banquet with apples and oranges, fresh butter, jelly glasses of red and yellow preserves, a basket of eggs which Susannah fancied were the last from the Plymouth Rocks, the pitcher of milk, the last from Kate's Jerseys. "I don't think I could eat anything," she said quietly.

"Sure you can, Missy! You all gotta git somethin' in your stomachs and git you some sleep." Abruptly Pepper held up her finger. "Oh, 'fore I forgits, Jason. Miles Sadler stopped in jest a little while ago lookin' for you."

"For me?"

"He got a message on his CB radio from that zoo feller in Oklahoma City."

Jason's shoulders fell. "He probably wants to know about the gaur."

"No, he know all about 'em. He say to tell you they's jest fine. They's back in the pen there and they's jest fine."

Jason scratched his head. "There must be some mistake."

"That what Miles said he told him, but the zoo feller said they got the right numbers tatooed on they ears and he really appreciate you seein' to it they got there safe and sound."

Jason sat down slowly, looking more and more bewildered. "There must be some mistake," he repeated. "That's a hundred and fifty miles."

"Maybe somebody picked them up," said Marty.

"Sure," said Susannah. "I can just picture it! 'Step into my truck here, you sweet little things. . .'"

"There must be some mistake," Jason said again.

"The Lord work in mysterious ways," said Pepper. "Now maybe I can go to the barn again to look for the settin' hens that ain't supposed to be settin', without them beasts snortin' fire at me. When we gits a new barn. When we gits new chickens."

"There must be a reasonable explanation," Jason insisted.

"They ain't nothin' unreasonable about it. Them wild things didn't belong here. They's gone back where they belongs. Mysterious ways—wondrous ways."

Jason shook his head. It was useless to argue with Pepper when she and God were in agreement. "A new barn, huh? New chickens? You certainly do move quickly, Pepper."

"Well, a body don't git work done by standin' around lookin' at it. The hands come in 'bout an hour ago and I give them some breakfast, told them they'd best git some rest 'cause they'd be needed later on at the house."

Jason smiled wearily. "I guess that means you have some plan of action?"

Pepper rubbed her chin thoughtfully. "Well, we needs the stuff out of the pantry. And clothes and beddin' if they is any. And whatever else we can use. Then I reckon you just start pickin' up the pieces." She lifted her shoulders in a gesture of helplessness. "I don't know what else a body's to do, Jason."

He turned and looked across the room to the sink where Kate had just washed her hands and held them out, dripping, while her eyes searched, in a confused and sleepy way, for a towel.

"You think we can do that, Kate?" he said, wondering if she heard.

She looked at him over the tops of her fingers held in front of her like those of a just-scrubbed surgeon, and her mind came under siege. A banner with the legend "Happy Ending" floated in the air above her, and she knew it immediately for an old vision, an old lie, just as the next banner, "Fresh New Start," was an old lie. Destroyed houses were shored up where possible, patched with the usables discovered in the ruins. New pieces, new elements were added at great expense to all concerned. Even a brand-new house built on top of cleared wreckage stood on the same old ground. Maybe not quite the same? Maybe? Maybe not? Whatever, she had to have the house so she could have the wall—a wall on which to hang Grandfather Sullivan. What was he like, this horseshoe pitcher? Who came to live again in her son? Eloquent and silver-tongued? They all were, weren't they—hiding the truth in the music of the words. Maybe he would hang on the new wall and look down on them with new words, new unspoken words, pure words, not messed over with all the associations of words known for such a long time.

She shook her hands, then wiped them down the front of her blouse. "Yes, Jason," she said firmly, meeting his look and holding it, "I would like to try to build a house."

Pepper watched them intently as they watched each

other, then looked past them to where Hodge leaned listlessly against the door, and her expression softened. She
went to him, placed a gently curious hand on his cast.
"Hurt?" she asked, and ran her fingers over it when he
shook his head that it didn't. She brushed his hair out of his
eyes and breathed deeply as one does before saying a difficult thing. "Lester wanted you to know. They buried your
horse. Lester thought you'd want that."

Hodge raised his head to find them all staring at him with
grieved expressions. "I'm much obliged," he said finally.
Then he looked at Pepper with a wan smile. "I guess I'll
have some breakfast," he said. "It's morning, isn't it?"

The sun was overhead in an innocent blue sky, the day
balmy and warm, when they started to work. Jason, Marty
and Page, with Lester and the other hands, went about the
business of felling what still stood and then collecting into
piles what could be used, and into other piles what Jason,
ruefully and repeatedly, referred to as kindling. Hodge directed Meg and Patrick as they prodded in the ruins,
searching, Meg thought, for treasure.

Kate and Susannah pulled canned goods from the pantry, what was left of it, then moved into what had been the
kitchen, finding little there to salvage.

"Maybe Jason can fix this," Susannah said as she studied
the chunks of the oak table from North Carolina.

Kate shook her head and dropped a jagged piece of Haviland onto a pile of splintered chestnut. "It makes me feel so
empty," she said. "Hollow. As if I wasn't really a person at
all, just the sum of my possessions." She looked around
her. "And there're precious little of those now."

"You have your family," Susannah reminded her. "All of
them safe."

Kate nodded agreement. "Except Page," she sighed.
"Page Garrity is unsafe. He should have a big sign hung
around his neck—'Danger: Explosive.'" She smiled at Susannah's questioning look. "He thinks the storm was my
fault, that God sent it to punish all of us for my—my
trespasses."

Susannah thought of Pepper in the cellar, demanding to know if she was the culprit. So there always had to be a villain in the piece? A perfectly natural, explainable catastrophe built out of wind and weather had to be assigned to a guilty party. Carnal knowledge, it would appear, could level the earth. Aloud she said, "He's angry, Kate, and hurt. Not to mention thirteen years old. Those are all things that people can get over."

Kate began to rummage again through the rubble at her feet. "I hope so," she said. "I do hope so." She glanced up with an expression that combined irony and mischief. "That's one of the chances you take when you have kids. They may get an unfair share of your own failings." She held up a copper pot—one that had hung for decades from a hook over the fireplace—inspecting its dents. "So what do you think about this?"

There was a sudden clatter behind them, and they both turned. Meg scrambled headlong over the boards that her mother quickly reminded her had nails in them, slowed for a moment, then dashed on in her excitement. Patrick followed, head down in his natural caution, and behind him Hodge, his gait made awkward by the burden of his right arm and by what he hugged in his left.

"Hodge found them!" Meg cried, jumping up and down. "Hodge found them out by the stables."

With a smile stretched across his face, Hodge came forward and offered, clumsily from the crook of his arm, the Meissen salt-and-pepper set, shining white and luminous through the rents in their coats of mud.

Kate took them and pressed them against her breast, closing her eyes on the tears that slipped from them. They all stood quietly for a time, until Meg and Patrick, bored with their mother's response, and Hodge, sensitive to it, returned to their treasure hunt.

Kate wiped her eyes on the tail of her blouse. "I'd like you to have them," she sniffed. "You asked for them once and I wouldn't give them to you. I want you to have them now."

Susannah shook her head. "No, they belong here. Gran's things came to you and for good reason."

Kate's face brightened with the light of a flashing thought. "Then we'll share them," she cried. "As long as they belong to us they're still a set."

Susannah's eyes opened wide. "Oh yes!"

Kate held them out. "Which one?"

Susannah hesitated and looked from one to the other. "Oh, I don't know—it doesn't matter, not really."

"Which one?" Kate insisted, her eyes glittering with excitement.

"Well, I guess I like the salt cellar best."

Kate blinked, her smile faded, her face closed down, and the hand that held Susannah's choice drew back, almost imperceptibly.

"What's wrong?"

"Nothing," Kate said sharply, and she handed over the salt cellar.

"This was your idea!"

"You *know* I love those swans."

"So keep it," Susannah snapped, thrusting it toward her. "Keep them both!"

They eyed each other as the old tenured headwind gusted and swirled about them, raw and sharp in spite of the efforts, earnest and merciful, of the past days. Then suddenly Kate made a strangled, coughing noise, her lips twitched, her shoulders jostled up and down, and she commenced to build a towering laugh. It started in her chest as a deep cackle, bellowed into her throat, where Susannah caught it, and came out a raspy, jubilant duet.

They took careful sideways steps off the rubble onto flat ground. Kate waved the pepper grinder in one hand and grasped her sister's shoulder with the other. Susannah shook the salt cellar like a witch doctor's gourd, then let out a savage howl as she seized Kate. Crouched low, like wary primeval animals, they began to circle in a slow, ceremonial dance, touching foreheads, engaging the great weapon inside, laughing . . . laughing.